WHAT DO REAL PIGEONS PECK?

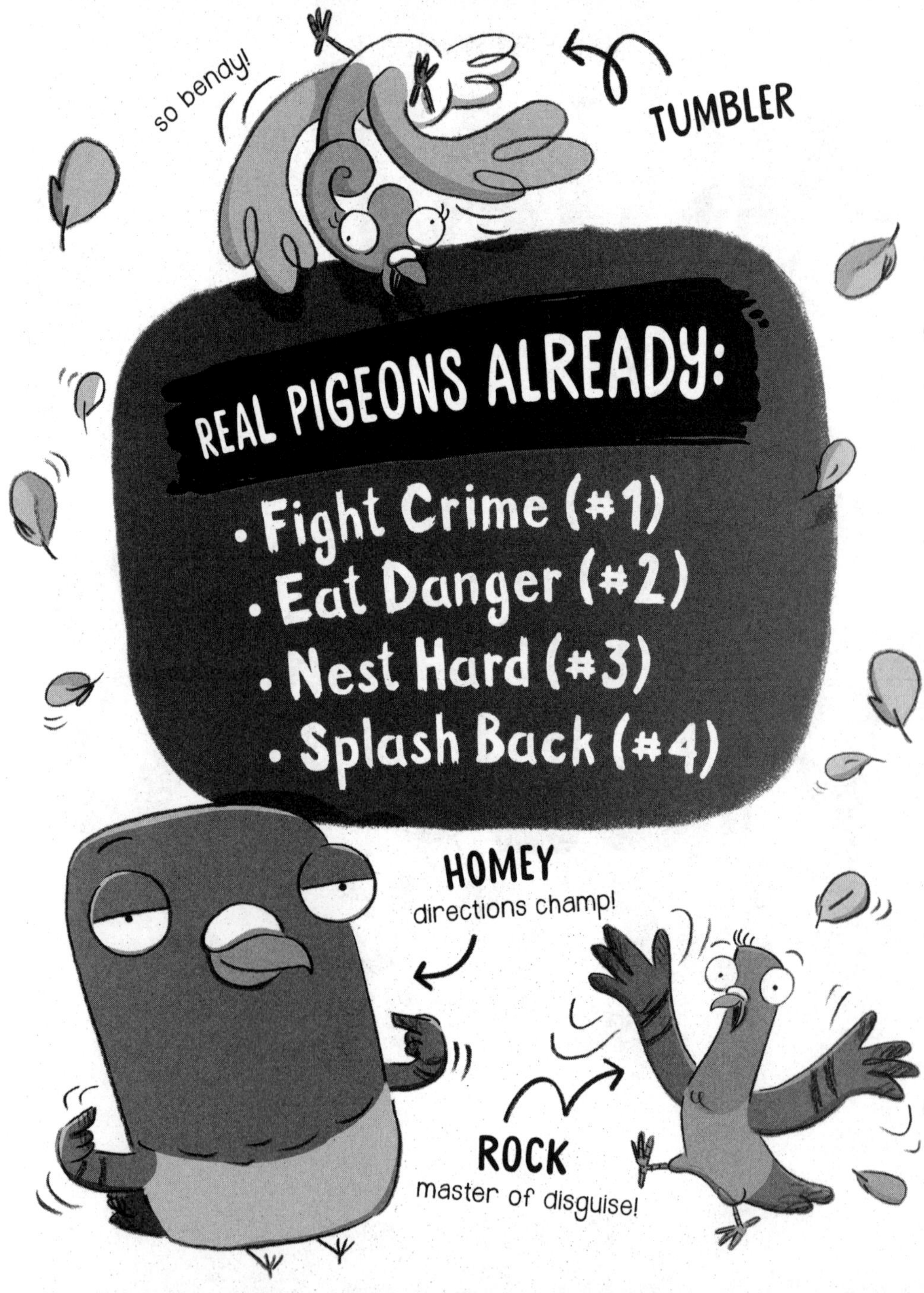
so bendy!
TUMBLER
REAL PIGEONS ALREADY:
• Fight Crime (#1)
• Eat Danger (#2)
• Nest Hard (#3)
• Splash Back (#4)
HOMEY
directions champ!
ROCK
master of disguise!

REAL PIGEONS

PECK PUNCHES

WITHDRAWN

← FRILLBACK
superstrong!

RANDOM HOUSE 🏠 NEW YORK

ANDREW McDONALD and BEN WOOD

CONTENTS

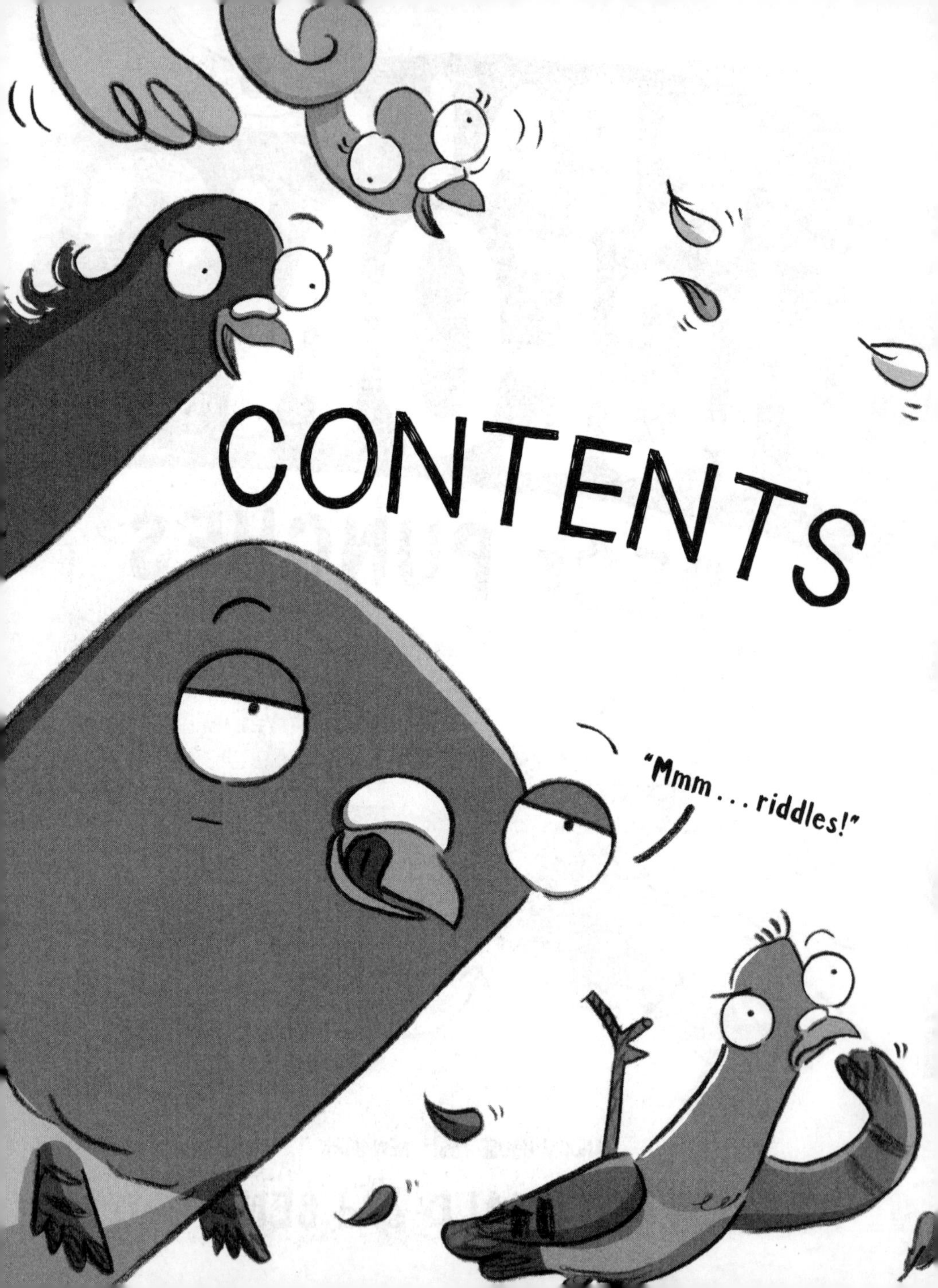
"Mmm . . . riddles!"

FOR HILARY ROGERS —ANDREW
FOR JANINE, SHONA, MAKAI, AND LEXON —BEN

Text copyright © 2020 by Andrew McDonald
Cover art and interior illustrations copyright © 2020 by Ben Wood
Series design copyright © 2020 by Hardie Grant Children's Publishing

All rights reserved. Published in the United States by Random House Children's Books, a division of Penguin Random House LLC, New York. Originally published in paperback by Hardie Grant Children's Publishing, Australia, in 2020.

Random House and the colophon are registered trademarks of Penguin Random House LLC.

Visit us on the Web! rhcbooks.com

Educators and librarians, for a variety of teaching tools, visit us at RHTeachersLibrarians.com

Library of Congress Cataloging-in-Publication Data is available upon request.
ISBN 978-0-593-42720-0 (hc) — ISBN 978-0-593-42722-4 (ebook)

Printed in the United States of America
10 9 8 7 6 5 4 3 2 1
First American Edition 2022

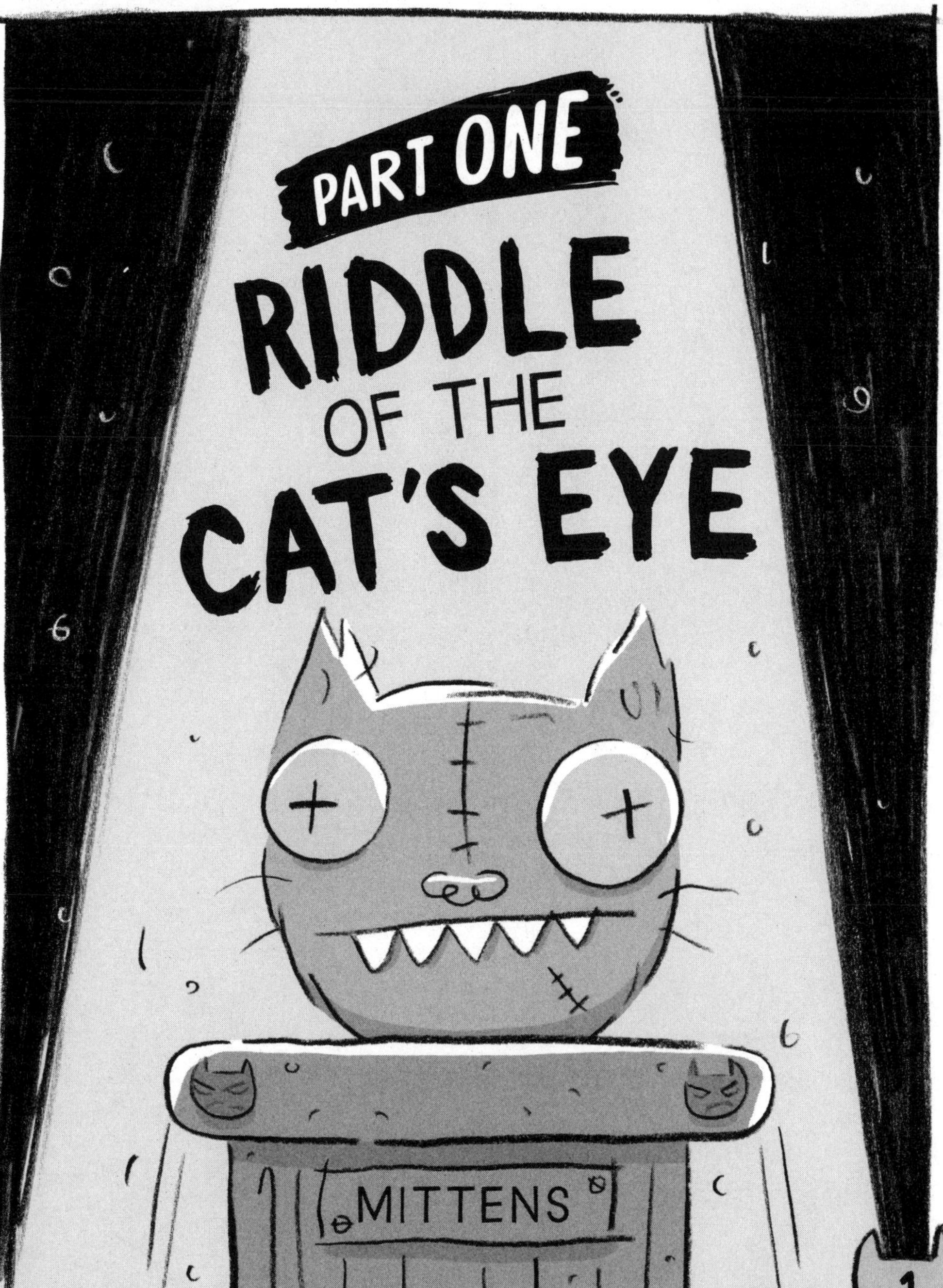
PART ONE
RIDDLE
OF THE
CAT'S EYE
MITTENS

CHAPTER 1

This is Earth.

It is home to some very special creatures.

"Me? Why, thank you!"

These creatures are smart, strong, and found all over the planet.

They are . . .

. . . PIGEONS!

"Hello!"

"Ugh, pigeons are so DIRTY."

Rock Pigeon always tries his best to be clean.

"I am NOT dirty!"

He avoids germy messes.

HOP!

He brushes inside his beak with his pet twig, Trent.

grass

SCRUB
SCRUB
SCRUB

And although he sometimes eats OLD food, it's only ever bread crumbs. They are good fresh OR stale.

"Bread doesn't go BAD. It only goes IN!"

Rock is part of a team of crime-fighting pigeons.

Each pigeon has a special **PIGEON POWER.**

Homey
(super good at directions)

Frillback
(super strong)

Tumbler
(super bendy)

Rock
(super good at costumes)

STRONG BODS

"Yay!"

Today, Rock is watching for crime while disguised as a magazine.

He isn't the only one watching.

All the city pigeons help too. Their **PIGEON POWER** is **SPYING**.

"Hmmmm."

"Hmm."

"Hmmm."

All these pigeons are part of . . .

It is a **NETWORK** because all the pigeons work together.

"Scooter thief!"

"Whee!"

"Gotcha!"

They are **WILD** because they don't have owners.

"Pigeons don't do leashes!"

CLICK!

"**BAD DOG.**"

8

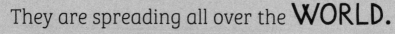
They are spreading all over the **WORLD**.

"The more **SPIES** we have, the better!"

"Let's **SPY** in Jamaica!"

"Hooray!"

And they are **REAL PIGEONS** because real pigeons don't just coo, peck, and poo—

REAL PIGEONS FIGHT CRIME!

Rock and Homey visit some city pigeons to see if they have other crimes to report.

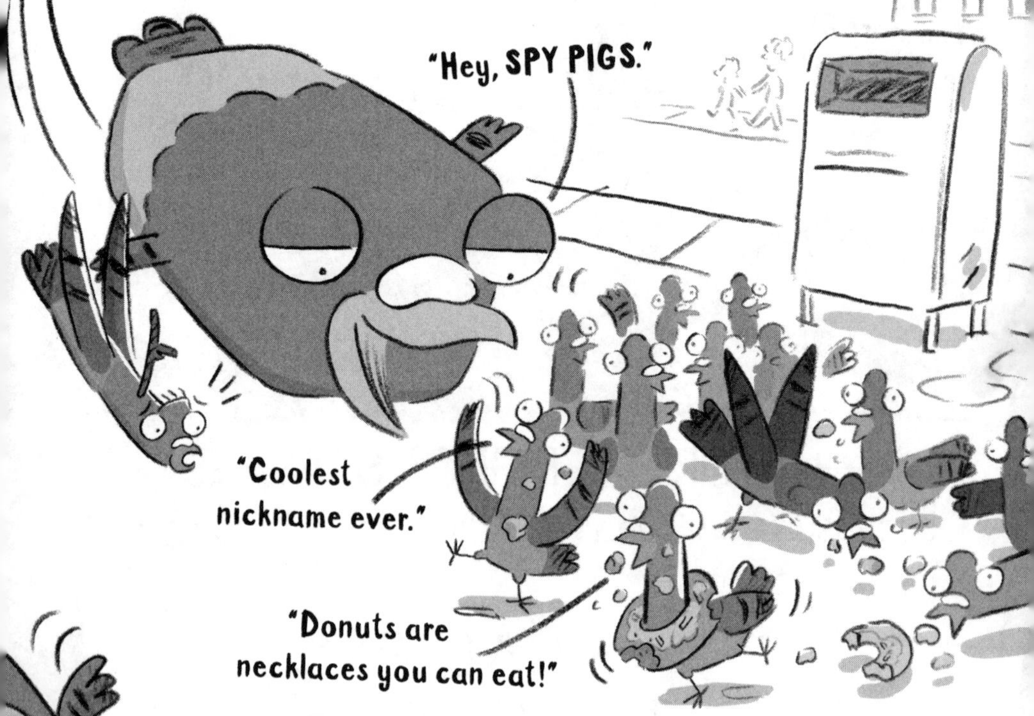
"Hey, SPY PIGS."
"Coolest nickname ever."
"Donuts are necklaces you can eat!"

Rock worries that the city pigeons are being dirty.

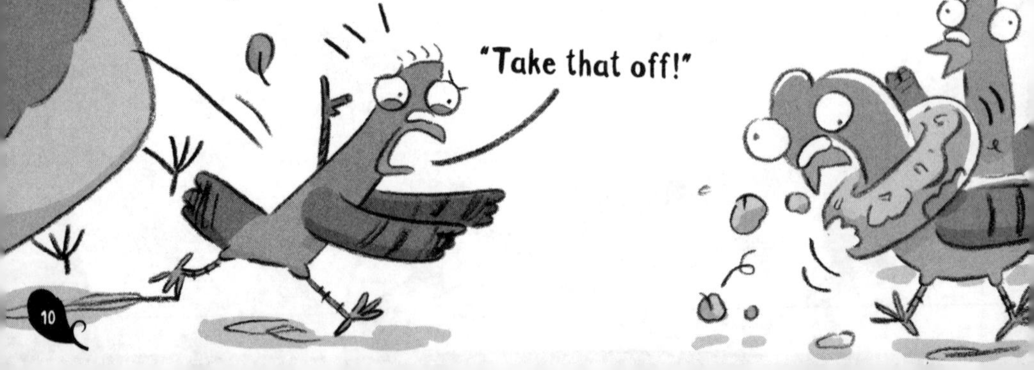
"Take that off!"

"Hello, boys," cries a voice from inside a mailbox.

"Barb Pigeon!" yelps Rock. "What are you doing in there?"

"Hi, Barb!"

"We love you, Barb."

"I live here now," says Barb. "Come in, dears." They fly in and join Barb for tea bags and bread crumbs.

"I wish all pigeons were as clean as you, Barb," says Rock. "Your feathers look so smooth. Anyway, have you seen any crime lately?"

"No, but I'm on the lookout," says Barb, peeking outside. "See, there's someone who is a danger . . . to herself!"

The pigeons all peer out and see a human walk past.

clumsy human

bee about to fly into mouth

hot coffee

DANGER! DO NOT ENTER

Rock has to do something.
Before the clumsy human
gets hurt.

"Quick,
Trent!"

He spots a lost
hankie on the
ground.

It's a bit grubby. But this
is an emergency!

He ties it around his neck.

It looks like a cape,
but it's actually . . .

...a **POCKET!**

Rock is a
**MASTER
OF DISGUISE.**

He stops the bee
from flying into the
human's mouth.

He stops her from spilling coffee on herself.

"Coffee tastes like hot mud puddles."

And he swats away a pickpocket.

SWAT
SWAT
SWAT

But the danger is not over yet.

DANGER!
BIG HOLE!

Luckily, Homey has gathered the others.
They swoop in to save the human.
By becoming a **PIGEON PLANK**.

But the human doesn't even notice, because she's on her phone.

"Hello, Bertie Berd-Byrd here," she says.

"What's that? There's been a crime at my museum?"

"Crime!" says Rock. "Finally."

"Someone has stolen the Cat's Eye emerald?" she cries. "My rare and priceless jewel!"

Bertie Berd-Byrd rushes off.

"Did she say CAT'S Eye?"

"We'd better tell Grandpouter," says Rock.

They speed off to their gazebo.

Grandpouter is the leader of the **REAL PIGEONS NETWORK**.

He has been teaching some city pigeons **MORSE COODE**. So they can talk in secret.

"Cooo. Coo coo coo coo. Coo cooo. Cooo coo. Cooo coo cooo. Coo coo coo."

"Are you wearing a dirty hankie?"

"Ew, I never thought of that!"

Rock removes the hankie. "We have a new case!" he cries.

"A Cat's Eye emerald has been stolen from the museum!" explains Tumbler.

"It's our duty to find the emerald and return it," says Grandpouter.

"REAL PIGEONS FIND STOLEN EMERALDS!"

"There are lots of **SPY PIGS** now," says Homey. "Could they solve this mystery so we can snooze for once?"

"Real Pigeons don't snooze!"
says Frillback. "Come on—
we need to start looking for clues."

"That's right," says Grandpouter.
"Who knows **WHERE** this
emerald might show—

"**COO-OUGH!**"

He suddenly coughs up
a shiny green stone.

CLUNK

CLUNK CLUNK

"Is that . . . the Cat's Eye
emerald?" cries Rock.

CHAPTER 2

The stolen Cat's Eye emerald is **RIGHT THERE**.

"We just solved the case in record time!" cries Homey.

SPARKLE SPARKLE

"It looks **EXACTLY** like a cat's eye," says Tumbler nervously.

Pigeons do not like cats.

Cats eat birds. And are cranky sourpusses.

But it's mostly the bird-eating thing.

"Where did it come from?" asks Rock.

Grandpouter gulps and points to the large bubble under his beak.

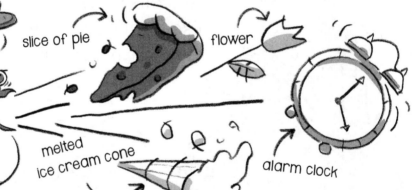

"The emerald was in my **CROP!**" he says. "Where I keep snacks to swallow later."

He coughs up a few more objects.

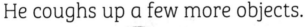

slice of pie

flower

melted ice cream cone

alarm clock

"But I have no idea how the emerald got in there!" he adds.

"And now we have another problem," says Rock.

Some baddies have noticed the Cat's Eye.

"Move toward the sparkling light!"

"A pretty jewel!"

"HISS HISS— my emerald!"

There are some moths, a lizard, and a . . .
"Is that a swan?" asks Frillback, confused.
"Or a snake pretending to be a swan?"

"I don't know," says Rock. "But swans
and snakes are always grumpy!"

"I don't like the SwanSnake!"
says Tumbler.

23

"We need to keep the Cat's Eye emerald safe," says Rock. "And return it to the museum."

Frillback shoves the Cat's Eye back into Grandpouter's beak and **FLY KICKS** the baddies away.

The pigeons zoom off.

"There are only three ways the Cat's Eye could have ended up in your **CROP**," Rock says to Grandpouter. "You might have accidentally eaten it."

"Yum yum!"

Grandpouter shakes his head. "I haven't eaten in days. Because I've had a pie in my crop."

"Then maybe your crop magically turns things into emeralds?" says Rock. "Let's check!"

The pigeons find old pieces of chewing gum on the street and shove them into Grandpouter's beak.

SHOVE

But when he coughs them up, they are sadly not emeralds.

PLOP

PLOP

PLOP

"So that's where chewing gum comes from!"

"There's only one other explanation," says Rock. "Someone must have PUT the emerald in your beak."

"Actually, I saw a shadowy figure near Grandpouter last night," says Frillback. "I thought I dreamt it."

"Someone wants to make it look like WE stole the emerald!" says Rock. "But who?"

Jungle Crow — #1 enemy of the Real Pigeons

Megabat — self-obsessed enemy of the Real Pigeons

InvisiFrog — invisible enemy of the Real Pigeons

"But why?"

"Hey, PIGS!" cries Homey. "Where did Tumbler go?"

Tumbler is just around the corner. She has found a coo new shop.

PIPE CLEANERS

"Pipe cleaners are super bendy—just like me."

But she does a curly scream when the **SwanSnake** pops out.

"HISS HISS!"

"AHHHHH!"

Suddenly, Tumbler is thrown into a dark bag.

Where a slimy monster punches her.

Luckily, she finds a way out.

PLOP!

Without looking back, Tumbler flees.

"I've been attacked!" she cries.

She tells the others what happened.

"And I still don't know if he was a swan or a snake!"

Frillback gives Tumbler a firm hug.

"It doesn't matter whether he's a **SWAN** or a **SNAKE**!" cries Frillback. "He tried to hurt you. Maybe he thought *you* had the Cat's Eye?"

"Back on the gazebo, the **SwanSnake** said the Cat's Eye was *his*," says Rock. "Maybe he stole it from the museum and wants it back."

"Then how did it get into my beak?" asks Grandpouter.

"I don't know."

The pigeons are puzzled.

"Think, Homey brain, think!"

"We need to return the Cat's Eye emerald before anyone else attacks us," says Rock. "We might need some . . . **PIGEON BACKUP!**"

The pigeons fly to Barb's mailbox
to find some city pigeons.
It is strangely quiet.

No pigeons
here

or here

or under
here!

"Where are the rest of the city pigeons?" asks
Rock. "There were *so* many here before."

Barb shrugs. "I have no idea."

"Well, can you three help us at the museum?" says Rock. "We're under attack and trying to return an emerald."

"Maybe another time."

"I can't—I have a feathercut booked."

"We don't like the museum much," says Barb.

"Oh. OK!"

The gang takes off again. Rock doesn't understand why those pigeons wouldn't help.

Until they arrive at the museum.

CAT MUSEUM

"It's not just any museum!" says Rock. "It's a . . . CAT MUSEUM!"

GULP!

34

No pigeon wants to visit a **CAT** museum.

Not even a **REAL PIGEON**.

But they can't leave the Cat's Eye on the museum doorstep. Not with everyone trying to steal it.

"We're just waiting for our chance!"

"There's got to be another way to return the emerald," says Rock.

They peer around a corner and see someone leaning out of a window, eating a burger.

SLOP
SLURP!

"It's that museum lady, Bertie Berd-Byrd!" cries Rock.

As Bertie goes back inside, the pigeons move to the ledge. It's covered in burger juice.

SPLOSH
SPLASH!

"Hey!" cries Rock. "You're all getting dirty!"

"Chill, dude," says Homey. "We can give the Cat's Eye straight to Bertie and get out of here."

They all peer inside.

"When the night guard arrives at the back door at nine, tell him to keep an extra eye out for the thief!"

"Yes, ma'am!"

LICK LICK

Bertie has a cat. But thankfully, he hasn't seen them yet.

"How will we get past that cat?" asks Grandpouter.

"Maybe we can disguise ourselves as feather dusters?" says Rock.

"Or feather earrings?"

"Hey, does anyone else smell something flowery, like shampoo?"

GRAB!

"AHHH!"

"Hello, pigeons!"

The cat grabs the birds with his tail. He laughs, and it sounds like claws scratching a blackboard.

"My name is Shampoo," says the cat. "Because I shampoo myself every morning. I believe in being **CLEAN!** But you are typical **DIRTY** pigeons."

"Actually, we're here to return—"

"You're wrong!" shouts Rock. "Pigeons are **NOT** dirty."

"Then why is your buddy licking up burger juice?" says Shampoo.

"HOMEY!"

"Technically, I'm **CLEANING** it up."

The cat leans forward and opens his mouth.
His white teeth glisten in the sun.

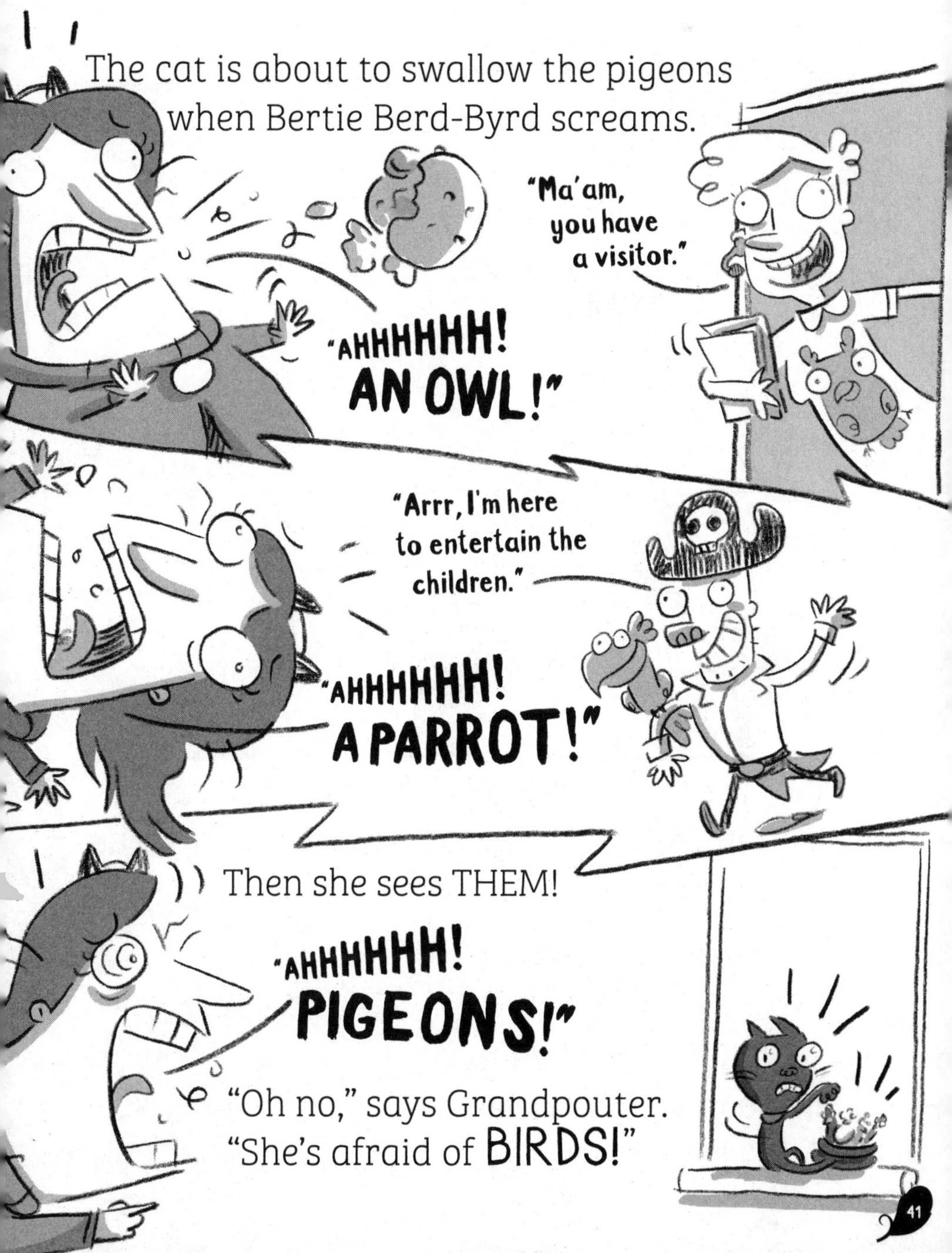
The cat is about to swallow the pigeons when Bertie Berd-Byrd screams.
"Ma'am, you have a visitor."
"AHHHHHH! AN OWL!"
"Arrr, I'm here to entertain the children."
"AHHHHHH! A PARROT!"
Then she sees THEM!
"AHHHHHH! PIGEONS!"
"Oh no," says Grandpouter. "She's afraid of BIRDS!"

She leaps over and slams the window down as the pigeons break free.

"I don't want birds **ANYWHERE** near my museum!"

Rock is relieved that they haven't been eaten. But returning the emerald is turning out to be quite hard.

"We'll just have to take the Cat's Eye into the **CAT MUSEUM!**" he says, trying to sound brave. "And I know how."

42

At nine o'clock, the night guard arrives at the museum's back door.

He enters, and the door is about to shut behind him . . .

. . . when his pocket flies off . . .

SSSSS

. . . and wedges the door open.

"This hankie is still dirty, but it's useful for disguises!"

The pigeons all sneak inside.

"Now, remember," says Rock, "we don't want anyone to know we were here. So don't make a mess. Let's be **CLEAN** birds!"

As they pass the gift shop, they find some glow-in-the-dark stickers. Rock sticks them onto Trent.

"It's Trent Flashlight!"

Then they set off to find where the Cat's Eye was stolen from.

As they turn into the main hall, the **REAL PIGEONS** get a bad feeling.

Because they are surrounded by

THE ENTIRE HISTORY OF CATS!

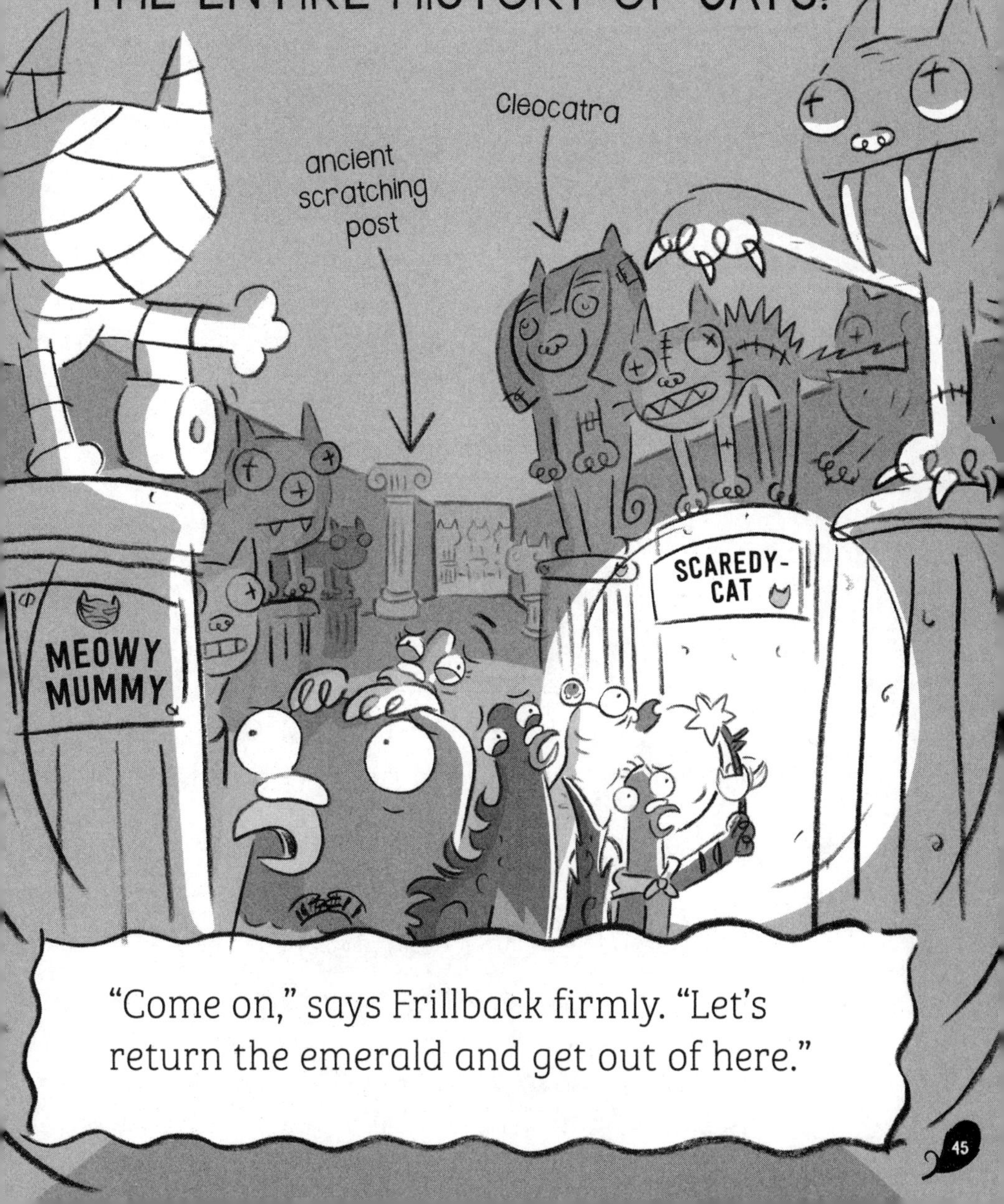
Cleocatra
ancient scratching post
MEOWY MUMMY
SCAREDY-CAT

"Come on," says Frillback firmly. "Let's return the emerald and get out of here."

Tumbler takes care of the security camera.

The pigeons zoom in and around lasers that detect movement.

And when a janitor wanders past, they blend into the background.

46

But the museum is big. They can't find an empty Cat's Eye display. And they're starting to make a mess.

"Homey! You're dropping bread crumbs everywhere."

"Grandpouter! You just coughed up some pie!"

"Rock! Boogers are dripping off your hankie!"

47

Luckily, Rock sees a sign.

He charges forward, lighting up the hallway with Trent Flashlight. "This way, gang."

But then he comes to a stop. Because towering over him . . .

is the SwanSnake!

"HISSSSS!"

RARE JEWELS THIS WAY

CHAPTER 4

"Hey!" yelps Rock nervously.
"Are you a swan or a snake?"

But the **SwanSnake** is in no mood to chat.
"I'll take my Cat's Eye back now, HISS
HISS, you DIRTY PIGEONS."

"We are NOT DIRTY!"
cries Rock.

"Of course you're **DIRTY**," says the **SwanSnake**. "You're wild animals, **HISS HISS!** You leave bread crumbs everywhere. You stand in burger juice. And you wear booger capes."

"It's a **POCKET** costume!"

Suddenly, Rock forgets about being scared. Because there's something wrong with the **SwanSnake's** beak.

"Is that fake?" he cries, lunging forward.

Rock grabs the beak, which comes right off. Then the eyes drop away. There's a familiar smell in the air.

"Get off, **HISS HISS!** You **DIRTY PIGEON.**"

"Rock, what are you doing?" shrieks Tumbler.

ROCK GIVES THE CREATURE AN ALMIGHTY TUG!

51

And pulls him completely into view.

The **SwanSnake** is actually . . .

Bertie Berd-Byrd's cat, Shampoo!

"Hello, dirty pigeons!"

"You're a **SwanSnakeCat!**" cries Rock.

The pigeons stare with wide-open beaks.

"Hey, I can open my mouth too!" Shampoo says. Then he grabs Rock and flings him into his jaws.

Rock has officially been **EATEN!**

A big pink tongue starts thrashing him.

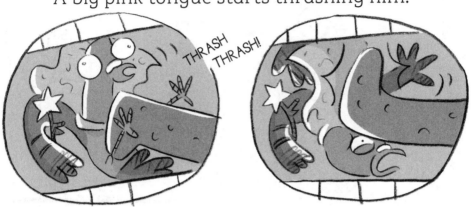

And wrestling with him.

"Hang on," says Rock. "Why am I only fighting a tongue? Why aren't I fighting teeth too?"

He pokes the cat's tongue with Trent.

The **SwanSnakeCat** spits Rock out.

PTOOEY!

"That hurt!" cries the cat.
"I was just trying to **CLEAN** you."

The pigeons stare at the cat.

"I thought you were trying to **EAT** me!" says Rock.

"I don't need to eat bony little pigeons," scoffs Shampoo. "Bertie feeds me tuna. I just want to clean everything."

"Were you cleaning me too?" gasps Tumbler.

"Of course," sniffs Shampoo. "Pigeons are the DIRTIEST. So I've decided to CLEAN you all! I use my tail as a distraction. Everyone is always so confused by a creature that could be a SWAN or a SNAKE."

Now Rock understands how Tumbler was attacked.

CLEAN CLEAN CLEAN

PLOP!

"Give me the Cat's Eye emerald!" says Shampoo.

"Why would we give it to **YOU?**" says Rock.

Shampoo sighs. "Because it's **MINE!**"

He points to a painting.

"I wear the emerald around my neck," he explains. "Bertie gave it to me when I was a kitten. It's priceless—to both of us!"

Rock realizes Bertie Berd-Byrd never said the emerald belonged to the *museum*.

"So how did it get into Grandpouter's crop?" says Rock.

"I did wake up a bit **DAMP** this morning," says Grandpouter. "You **CLEANED** me when I was asleep, didn't you?"

The cat shrugs. "I was seeing if it was easier to clean sleeping pigeons. I think my Cat's Eye fell into your beak then."

LICK
LICK
LICK

SNORE!

At once, Grandpouter coughs up the emerald.

"COO-OUGH!"

SPARKLE
SPARKLE

"Thank you," says Shampoo, happily fixing it back onto his collar. "Now there's just one thing to do. You pigeons need to be properly CLEANED UP!"

"Wait! What?"

"Again?"

Shampoo grabs a vacuum cleaner from the shadows.

"You're too dirty for Bertie's museum!" cries the cat. "So it's time to polish you off."

VROOM!

Before the pigeons can even flap, they disappear into the vacuum cleaner.

Rock is the last one to be sucked up. But Trent stops him.

TWANG!

"Trent, you beautiful wooden baby!"

"You know, I think you're right," says Rock to the cat. "We are DIRTY sometimes. Like, RIGHT NOW!"

"Huh?"

Rock pushes the vacuum's REVERSE button.

"NO! STOP!"

The pigeons are

BLASTED BACK OUT!

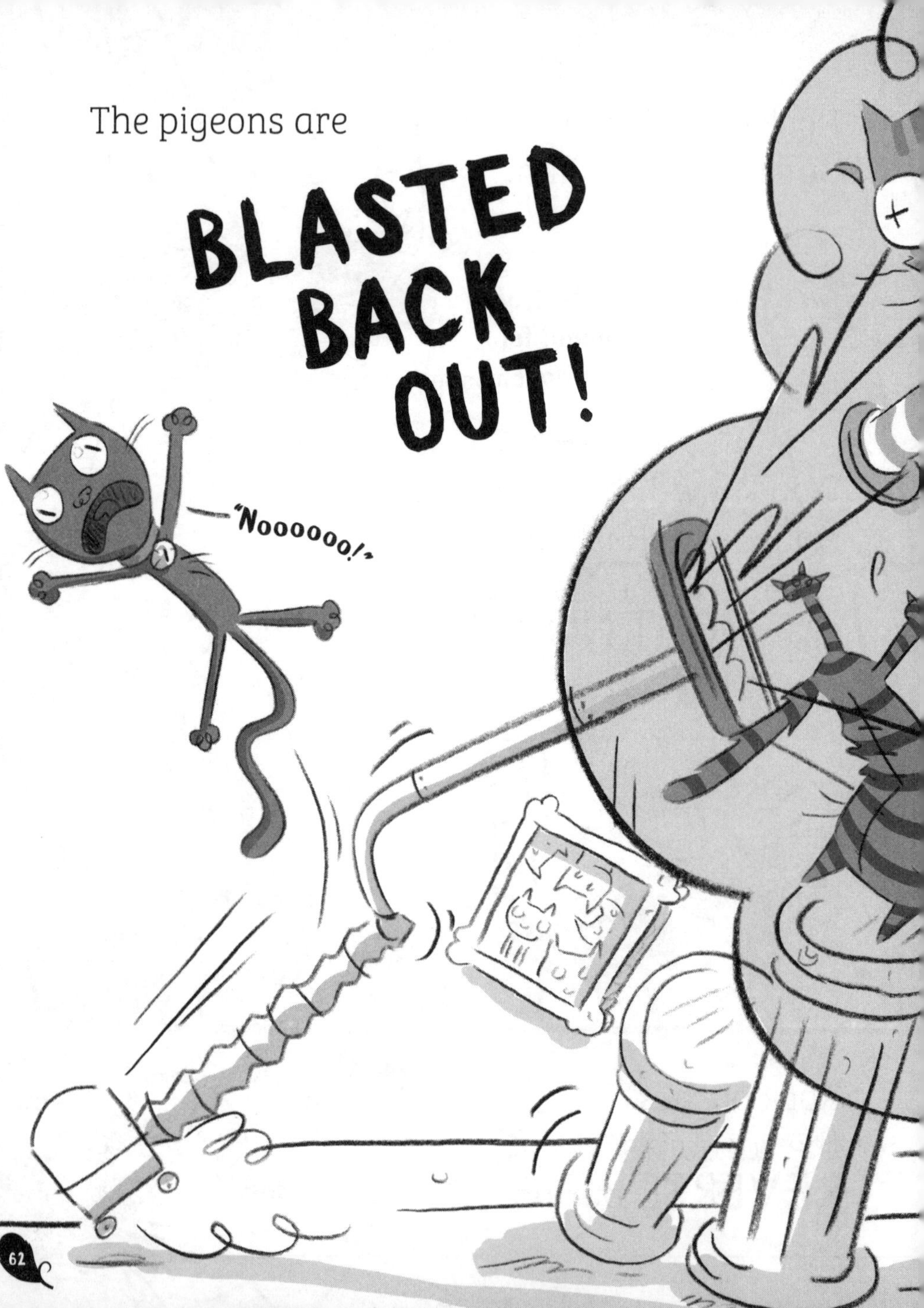
"Noooooo!"

Along with a huge cloud of dirt, dust, hair, fingernails, crumbs, and dried-up boogers.

Rock has made the CAT MUSEUM totally filthy.

"Dirt has saved the day," says Rock. "I love dirt now!"

The pigeons push open a window and fly into the night.

The riddle of the Cat's Eye is solved. And they're finally out of the museum.

So they celebrate . . .

. . . by getting completely DIRTY!

THE END

THE NEXT MORNING...

BERTIE BERD-BYRD LOOKS AT THE DAMAGE.

"Ma'am, we've discovered feathers from five different pigeons. They clearly broke in just to make a mess."

"I'm glad you found the emerald, Shampoo," she says. "But this is a CATASTROPHE."

MEANWHILE . . .

Barb Pigeon is wandering through the park with two city pigeons.

They walk up to a family of humans.

Barb lifts the edge of their picnic blanket.

The humans and the picnic are **FAKE**.

And underneath is a secret cave.

It is full of trapped city pigeons!

"Help us! Help!"

Barb pushes the last two pigeons in with the rest.

Then she pulls the fake picnic family back over the cave. And takes off her head.

She isn't Barb at all. She is **JUNGLE CROW,** the **REAL PIGEONS'** number one enemy!

"Stage One of my plan is complete! I won't be in this felt costume much longer. And the **REAL PIGEONS** won't be around much longer either. MWAHAHA!!"

TO BE CONTINUED ...

PART TWO THE
KAKAPO
CASE

CHAPTER 1

This is Homey.

He has an amazing **PIGEON POWER**.
He knows how to fly anywhere in the world.

But there's something he
likes better than flying.

LYING FLAT ON THE GROUND!

He is chilling outside his favorite bakery.

It's his favorite because humans always drop bread crumbs here.

"Is that pigeon sick? Have a snack, buddy!"

"Woo-coo!"

Meanwhile, Rock and Frillback are fighting crime and helping creatures.

"Come back here with that painting!"

"Hey, careful!"

"HELP!"

They fly over to check on Homey.

"What are you doing?"

"Hey, **PIGS**," says Homey. "I'm just chilling with a crumb!"

"If you chill too much, you'll forget how to fight crime!" says Frillback.

"Nah," says Homey. "You **PIGS** have got this."

"Just don't get lazy!" says Frillback, taking off.

"I'm not lazy!" yells Homey. "There's just no point flapping around if *everyone else* is fighting crime."

But Rock and Frillback have gone.

"Maybe I should have stood up to yell that?"

Homey finishes his snack.

"That bread crumb was delicious," he says. "I would rate it an **A**. Because it was **A** bread crumb and now I need another."

Two pigeons suddenly swoop down.

"Hi, PIGS!"

"Hello," they cry. "We're new to the **REAL PIGEONS WORLD WILD NETWORK** and we need your help!"

"Now it's my time to shine by fighting crime!" says Homey. "What's wrong?"

The pigeons coo in his ears.

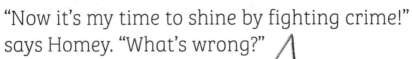

"Coo cooo.
Coo cooo coo. Coo cooo. Coo cooo coo. Coo.
Cooo coo cooo. Coo cooo. Cooo coo cooo. Coo cooo. Coo cooo cooo coo. Cooo cooo cooo.
Cooo coo coo coo. Coo coo. Coo cooo coo. Cooo coo coo.
Coo coo. Coo coo coo.
Coo coo. Cooo coo.
Cooo. Coo cooo coo. Cooo cooo cooo. Coo coo cooo.
Cooo coo coo coo. Coo cooo coo coo. Coo."

Pigeons all over the network have been learning to speak in **MORSE COODE**. That way, their messages are secret.

"Oh no!" cries Homey. "This is terrible."

The pigeons nod furiously.
"Yes, it's very terrible!"

"No, it's terrible that I can't remember how
MORSE COODE works," says Homey.
"I have no idea what you just said."

They all fly to the gazebo so Homey can check
the instructions.

"You were saying a rare
bird called Kakapo is in
trouble," says Homey.
"That IS terrible!"

"Exactly," says a pigeon. "We live in a distant land where lots of creatures want to eat Kakapo. We've been helping him hide. But it's getting too hard."

"Don't worry, PIGS," says Homey. "I know how to fly ANYWHERE. I'll rescue Kakapo!"

The pigeons give Homey directions, and he flies off.

He glides across the ocean.

Stops on a small island to refuel.

"Mmm, coconut bread!"

GONE FISHING

And finally finds Kakapo eating moss.

"Hey, dude!" cries Homey.
"Want to be rescued?"

"MUNCH MUNCH MUNCH!"

Kakapo agrees. But kakapos can't fly.

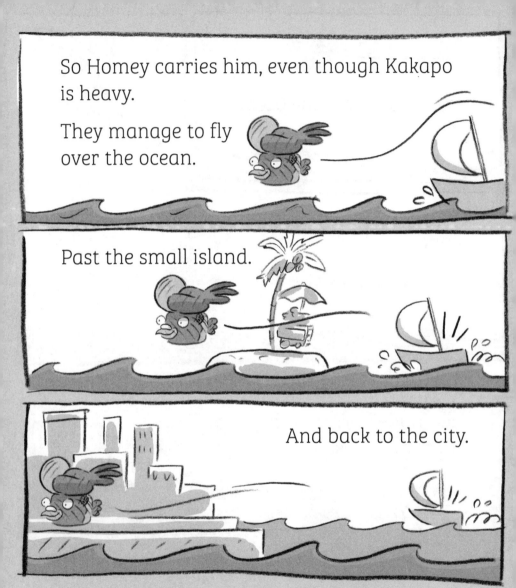

So Homey carries him, even though Kakapo is heavy.

They manage to fly over the ocean.

Past the small island.

And back to the city.

Homey looks over his shoulder. "I hope no one has followed me!"

By the time they reach the city, Kakapo has fallen asleep.

So Homey decides to hide him somewhere safe, and find the **REAL PIGEONS**.

But he doesn't notice the shadowy figure watching from the dock.

After hiding Kakapo, Homey joins the others in a pine tree. Pigeons can hang out anywhere. But they still love good old **TREES!**

"It's wonderful to get away and enjoy some fresh tree air!"

"Tree branches are the original window ledges."

"**PIGS!** I have something to tell you!" cries Homey.

Before Homey opens his beak, he checks that no one else is listening.

Then he whispers, "I've just rescued a **KAKAPO!**" He explains everything.

How Kakapo couldn't fly.

How he loves eating moss.

And all the important details.

"Seriously, you've got to try coconut bread!"

Rock's eyes grow wide.

"I've always wanted to meet a kakapo," he cries. "But there aren't many left in the world. I just wish they weren't so **ENDANGERED**."

big head

flappy wings

green feathers

"That's why I put him in **WITNEST PROTECTION**," says Homey. "So he doesn't witness a crime. The crime of being eaten."

"But what should we do with him now?" asks Tumbler.

The gang cries out:

"Coo cooo coo. Coo.
Coo cooo. Coo cooo coo coo.
Coo cooo cooo coo. Coo coo.
Cooo cooo coo. Coo. Cooo cooo cooo.
Cooo coo. Coo coo coo.
Cooo cooo cooo coo. Coo cooo coo.
Cooo cooo cooo. Cooo. Coo.
Cooo coo cooo coo. Cooo.
Coo cooo. Coo cooo. Cooo coo cooo.
Coo cooo. Coo cooo cooo coo.
Cooo cooo cooo."

Which is **MORSE COODE** for:

"REAL PIGEONS PROTECT KAKAPO!"

"Now, where did you hide him?" asks Rock.

Homey grins. "I hid him in the safest place in the city. Which, of course, is—"

87

At that moment, a pine cone falls on Homey's head.

PINE CONE CLUNK

"Homey!"

"Are you OK?"

"What are we all doing in this tree?" says Homey, sounding groggy.

"You were about to tell us where Kakapo is," says Grandpouter nervously.

Homey has never been more confused. "What is a kakapo?"

CHAPTER 2

Grandpouter tests Homey's memory.

"What is two plus two?"

"Four!"

"What do you eat for dessert after bread?"

"Bread!"

"Where did you hide Kakapo?"

"I don't know!"

Homey can't remember anything from the past day. The pigeons explain about Kakapo.

Homey shakes his head. "The last thing I remember is . . . Frillback saying that if I chill too much, I'll forget how to fight crime."

"Oh no!" Frillback grabs Homey's wings. "We'll fix this. You just chill. If you remember how."

"Don't worry, Frillbo!" he says with a grin.

"I haven't lost my chill."

"Have I?"

"Did you just call me *Frillbo*?"

Homey is worried. Deep down, he isn't chill
AT ALL.

Kakapo is lost because of him.

He needs to solve this mystery to get his
chill back!

"We'll have to find Kakapo with detective work," says Grandpouter. "Homey said he hid Kakapo in the safest place in the city. Where would that be?"

"Let me think."

Frillback jumps in. "Food is Homey's safe place! So maybe he hid Kakapo somewhere with lots of moss to eat."

Homey shrugs. "It's possible."

"Yes!" cries Rock. "And Homey knew Kakapo couldn't fly. So Kakapo must be somewhere *mossy* on the *ground*."

The birds split up to look for Kakapo.

WHOOSH!

WHOOSH!

WHOOSH!

Rock and Homey search in the town square. Weirdly, there are no other pigeons around.

"Where are all the city pigeons?"

"Maybe they discovered the joys of lying flat on the ground."

They visit lots of low, mossy parts of the city,
including . . .

A mossy rock.

A rocky moss.

And a mossy mouse.

There is no sign of Kakapo.

But they do find someone else.

It's Barb Pigeon.

She is near some humans who are having a picnic.

"Hello, Homey. Hello, Rocky. Hello, Trenty!"

"What are you doing, Barb?" says Rock.

"I was just . . . seeing if I could get a crumb from those people," Barb answers. "But, er, they gave me . . . um . . . evil glares."

"That's weird." Rock squints at the picnic. "They don't look evil to me. By the way, have you seen any other pigeons around?"

"Don't worry about that," says Barb, leading Rock and Homey away. "What little mystery are you dears investigating today?"

"I hid an endangered kakapo who loves eating moss, but then a pine cone fell on my head and I forgot where I hid him. But I haven't forgotten how to solve mysteries, you know!"

"Of course you haven't, my dear!"

Rock stops suddenly. "Homey, what if you didn't *hide* Kakapo? Maybe you just **DISGUISED** him!"

Rock leaps forward. "If I take off this squirrel's head, it might be **KAKAPO!**"

"Hey!"

"Or maybe this dog is really Kakapo?"

"The only thing you'll find in there is a **BARK!**"

"Or maybe Barb is really Kakapo?"

Rock reaches for Barb.

"**Wait!**"

"Homey isn't the master of disguise!" says Barb quickly. "But I know how you can find Kakapo."

"How?" wails Homey.

"Moss grows in dark, wet places," says Barb. "And so do mushrooms. Maybe you hid him at the mushroom shop!"

"I know that place, **PIGS**," says Homey, grabbing Barb. "Let's go!"

"I really shouldn't —"

"But we need you, Barb!"

The yard behind the mushroom shop is **FULL** of moss.

MAKE ROOM IN YOUR
MOUTH ROOM FOR
MUSHROOMS

"You were right, Barb!" cheers Rock.

"Mushrooms look like umbrellas that got cursed by a witch!"

The pigeons start searching for Kakapo.

They look **EVERYWHERE.**

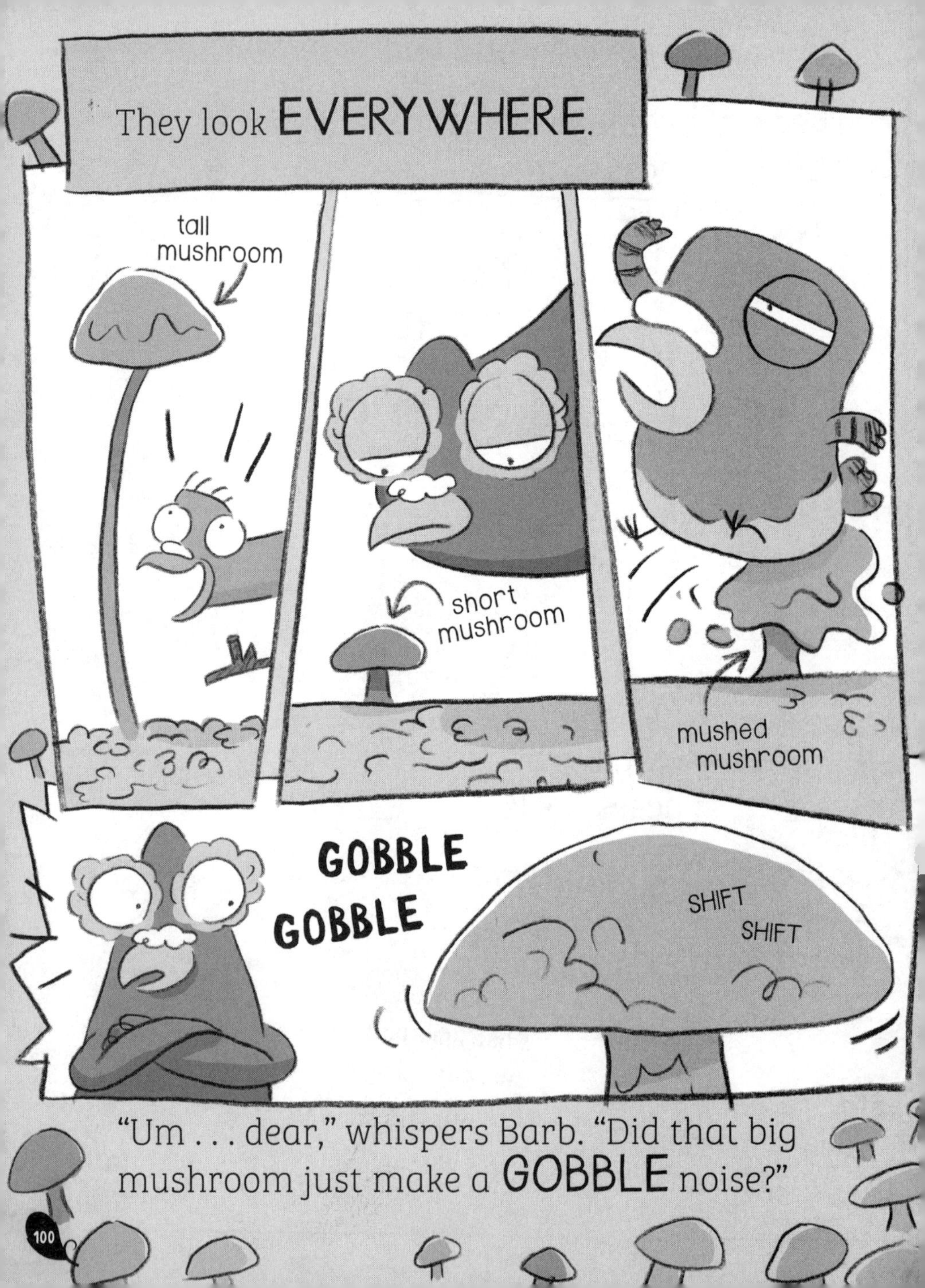
tall mushroom
short mushroom
mushed mushroom
GOBBLE
GOBBLE
SHIFT
SHIFT

"Um . . . dear," whispers Barb. "Did that big mushroom just make a **GOBBLE** noise?"

Homey, Rock, and Barb inch
closer to the mushroom.

"Maybe Kakapo is inside?" breathes Rock.

"I hope so!" says Homey, crossing his feathers.

Rock reaches over and lifts the mushroom's
head off.

But it's just a slug.

"Put that lid back on! The sun is hot, and I'm not wearing any slugscreen!"

"Sorry!"

As Rock replaces the lid, someone speaks behind them, in a voice that is squeaky AND evil.

"Hello, Homey!"

The pigeons spin around and gasp.

It's a weasel.

"I've been following you for a long time," he squeaks. "Now tell me where Kakapo is—or I'll eat your feathers, bones, and beaks before you can say *PIGS!*"

CHAPTER 3

Homey can't believe it.

"You've been hunting Kakapo?" he cries.

"I am **Ermine**," says the weasel, sucking his thumb. "And I will not rest until I have **EATEN** him."

SUCK
SUCK

"But he's endangered," gasps Rock.

A mean smile creeps up **Ermine's** face. "Yes," he sneers. "I want to taste him before he goes extinct."

"I stole a boat when I saw Homey rescue him. And I've been following you ever since."

"Why are you sucking your thumb?" says Barb.

"Because I am starving!" screeches **Ermine**. "I've been hunting **KAKAPO** for *weeks*. I am saving my big hunger for him. *Where is he?*"

"I've forgotten," says Homey. He is starting to get a bad feeling in his tummy. "But even if I did know, I'd never tell you!"

"As if I believe that," snarls **Ermine**. "Whatever, I'll find him. You don't look smart enough to win a game of hide-and-seek."

Homey's bad feeling isn't hunger. It's guilt! He can feel himself starting to freak.

"I'll be right back, **PIGS**," he says.

"Are you OK?"

"Everything is coo!" says Homey.

But he wanders around a corner and **FREAKS OUT.**

Because he hasn't saved Kakapo. He has put Kakapo in danger.

Then—**FREAK OUT** over—he returns.

"Sorry about that, **PIGS**," he says. "Where were we?"

"I think you **DO** know where Kakapo is," says **Ermine**. "So I am going to hang out with you. You'll visit Kakapo eventually."

He sucks his thumb and grins.

SUCK
SUCK

"Barb, can you fetch Frillback?" whispers Rock. "We're going to need her super strength."

"Sigh. I mean, sure!"

108

Rock and Homey try to get rid of **Ermine**.

Finally, the weasel gets distracted.

"If these chips were **KAKAPO**-flavored, we could end this right now!"

The pigeons fly off fast! Now they can concentrate on finding Kakapo.

They fly into Frillback in midair. "Barb told me you needed help!" she cries.

They are filling her in when they see **DANGER**.

old duck

distracted driver

speeding van

A terrible accident is about to happen!

This is the perfect chance for Homey to prove he isn't just good at chilling. He's good at fighting crime too.

"I'll save the day!"

He flies into the van and snatches the driver's lettuce sandwich.

CHOMP

The driver swerves just in time.

The van misses the old duck.
Hits a fire hydrant.
And water shoots everywhere,
along with some rats who
were swimming underground.

"Wheee!"

"I'm surfing and skydiving!"

Homey has saved the day! Right?

"Homey, this is a mess! You should have just chilled and let me sort it out!" says Frillback.

Homey pauses mid-chomp. "I wanted to prove I can still fight crime."

Rock frowns. "And you wanted to eat a lettuce sandwich."

"Lettuce is the shower curtain of sandwiches — thin, but important for separation."

Homey doesn't want to admit it, but inside his belly, he knows Rock has a point.

"Is it possible that you hid Kakapo in a place where you could also eat bread?" asks Rock.

Frillback's eyes go big. "The bakery!"

Homey shrugs. "It's possible."

"The bakery." **Ermine** laughs, leaping onto the rooftop. "Thanks for the tip."

"NO!"

Ermine has been secretly following them. He has heard everything!

The weasel slinks off in a flash. "I have a kakapo to eat!"

Rock and Frillback are about to chase him. But then Homey **FREAKS OUT** again. And this time he can't hide it.

Freaking out is tiring. So he lies down.

Rock and Frillback are concerned.

"Homey, it's going to be OK," says Rock, giving him a hug. "We'll find Kakapo together."

Frillback nods. "We just need to get to the bakery before **Ermine** does. Which way is it?"

Homey sits up. "I might not be the best crime-fighter. But I am **DEFINITELY** a directions champ!"

He takes off, zigzagging through the streets.

He's determined to save Kakapo for real this time.

When they arrive at the bakery, Barb is there.

"You always pop up just when we need you most, Barb!"

"Oh, it's you again."

Rock wonders why Barb is acting so strangely. But there's no time to find out.

Frillback reaches for Barb. "We need all the wings we can get."

But just as they're about to go inside the bakery, something gray flashes past.

Followed by another one.

And another.

"Are they tiny airplanes?" cries Rock.

"I bet they belong to **Ermine**," says Homey angrily. "He's trying to stop us from getting into the bakery!"

The gray flashes dip and dive everywhere.

The pigeons can't get past. Even the humans are running away scared.

"Help!"

"All I wanted was pumpkin bread!"

And Homey has a terrible thought.

What if **Ermine** is already inside— with Kakapo?

CHAPTER 4

Frillback quickly makes a wing-roof, and they all hide under it.

"I'll see you later."

"Not yet — we need you!"

Homey feels defeated.

Ermine is just too clever. He's outwitted them at every stage.

If only Homey could remember where he hid Kakapo.

He loves bread crumbs. But Homey would never put Kakapo in danger just to have a snack.

And didn't he say he hid Kakapo in the safest place in the city?

Homey's eyes grow as big as bread loaves.

"I know where I hid Kakapo," he cries. "And it's not the bakery."

"It's time to beat it," says Rock. "And by IT, I mean OUR WINGS!"

"Follow me, PIGS!" Homey shouts.

The pigeons speed through the city.

"Are you sure?"

"I'm pretty sure."

They land in the arms of the big old pine tree.

Grandpouter and Tumbler are there, waiting.

"Hi!"

Homey spreads his wings wide.

"PIGS, I **DID** hide Kakapo in the safest place in the city," he says. "And everyone knows the safest place is wherever the **REAL PIGEONS** are."

"What are you saying, Homey?" says Rock.

"Did you hide Kakapo in my feathers?"

"Did I wrap myself around Kakapo and not notice?"

"I'll bet I hid Kakapo in this very tree," says Homey. "Because this is where you all were."

The pigeons look all over the tree.

Between branches.

Under leaves.

Until there's only one place left to check.

Homey flies up to the wasp's nest at the very top of the tree.

He tips it over.

Homey is about to make a huge discovery.

OR get very stung.

Thankfully, there are no wasps.

Just a large green bird.

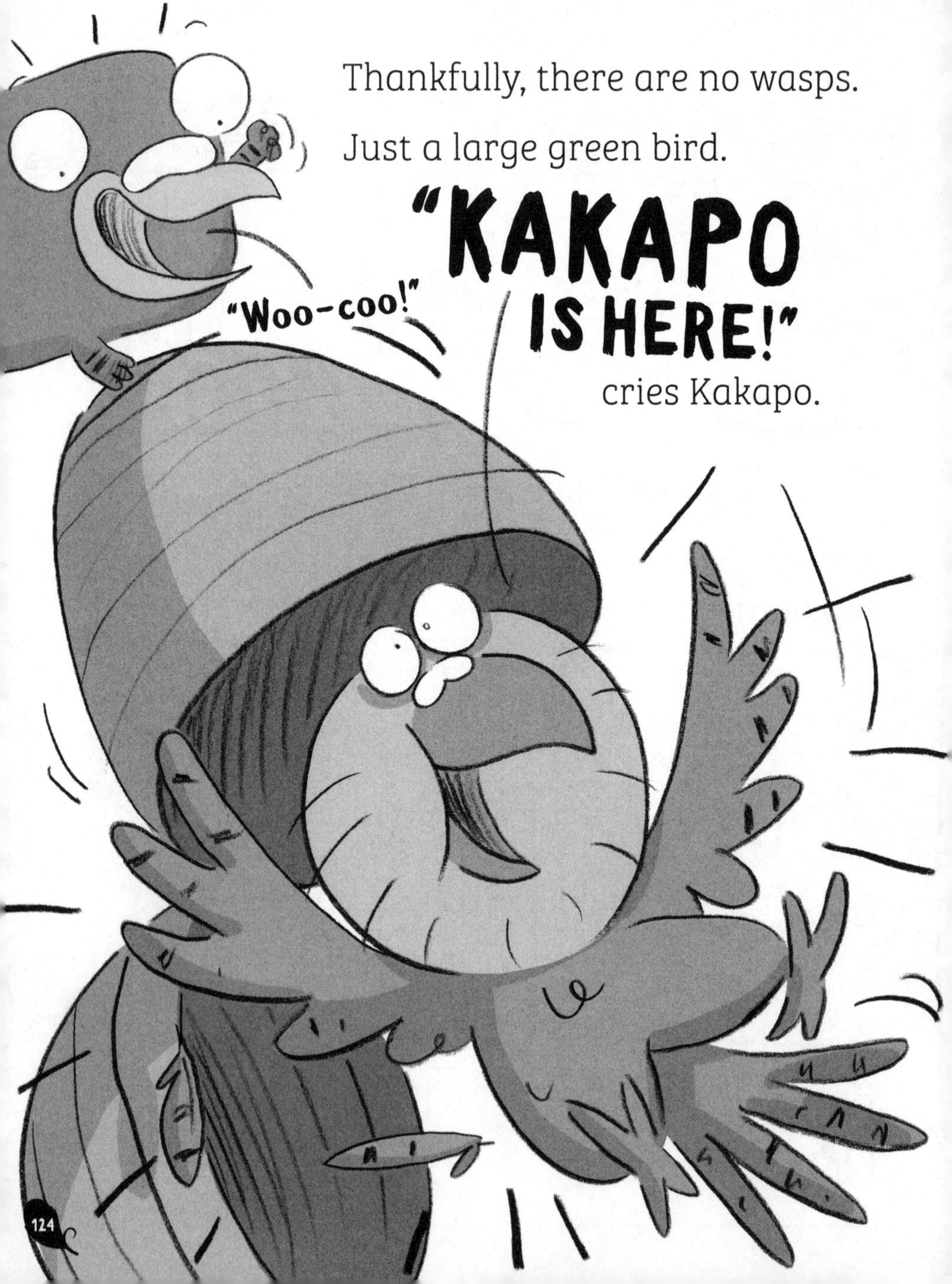
"KAKAPO IS HERE!"
"Woo-coo!"

cries Kakapo.

Kakapo is so excited he falls backward.

But Homey is there to cushion every bump.

"What fun!"

BRANCH BUMP

"I'm riding a roller coaster!"

TWIG THWACK

"Eeeeeeeeee!"

WOOD SPLINTER

After many bumps and thwacks, they land on the ground.

Kakapo sits there in a slight daze. Then he throws his wings in the air.

"Kakapo is OK!" He giggles. "Thank you for saving me, Pillow Bird!"

Homey smiles.

"You're welcome, Kakapo."

But a weaselly arm reaches around the tree trunk . . .

126

... and seizes Kakapo.
It's **Ermine**.

"Finally!" he screams in a fever of excitement. "I will eat you!"

The **REAL PIGEONS** freeze.

Grandpouter is speechless.

Tumbler is a knot of worry.

Frillback knows her super strength won't stop **Ermine** from eating Kakapo.

Rock is out of ideas.

Can Homey do something?

The weasel laughs and turns to Kakapo. "Now I will taste extinction. And I can stop sucking my thumb."

"No, you won't," says Homey. "Because I have a plan to stop you **AND** your tiny, flashy planes."

Ermine tilts his head in confusion. "What planes?"

At that moment, a pine cone falls from way above and hits the weasel on the head.

PINE CONE CLUNK

Ermine is out cold.

"That's a relief!" says Homey. "Because I had no plan."

Homey and Frillback pick up **Ermine**.

"I admire you, Homey," says Frillback. "You are so brave **AND** so chill! I wish I was like that."

"Thanks, Frillbo!"

129

Together they carry **Ermine** out of the city.

Over the ocean.

And leave him on an island for a long time-out.

"I'm actually JEALOUS of you. Coconut bread is incredible!"

GONE FISHING

With **Ermine** gone, all the birds reunite.

Even Barb comes. "Maybe we should have a **PICNIC** to celebrate?"

"Even better idea," says Kakapo happily. **"DANCE PARTY!"**

"Heel and toe! To and fro! Kakapo!"

THE END . . . FOR NOW

HOWEVER...

While the dance party continues, Grandpouter pulls Rock aside.

DANCE
DANCE
DANCE

GRAB!

"Rock, there's something you need to see," he says.

He takes Rock around a corner.

"What? No! That's not possible!"

Back at the dance party, Tumbler suddenly wraps herself around Barb.

"Hey! What are you doing?"

Rock steps forward.

And pulls off Barb's head.

133

Rock and his friends can't believe it.

All this time, Barb Pigeon has really been **Jungle Crow!**

"So you figured it out," sneers Jungle Crow. "How did you know?"

Another pigeon steps out from behind a branch.

It's the **REAL** Barb Pigeon.

This is what Grandpouter showed Rock.

"I've been on a cruise," says the real Barb Pigeon. "You get the best scraps on cruise ships! But now I'm back. And I hear someone has been pretending to be me!"

135

"I should have known." Rock frowns.

"I hope you enjoyed your cruise," says Jungle Crow. "Because my plan is almost complete. There's just one thing left to do."

Just then, some gray flashes zoom over.

They aren't tiny planes at all.

"REAL PIGEONS—meet my ROBOT PIGEONS!" Jungle Crow snickers.

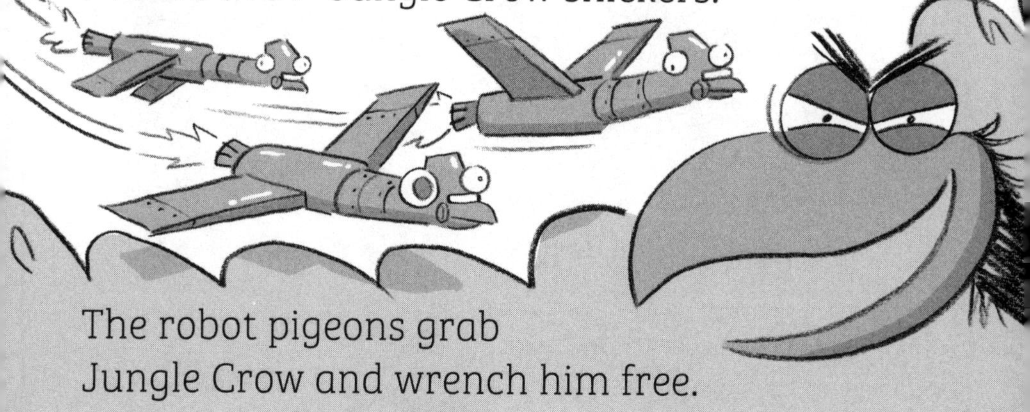

The robot pigeons grab Jungle Crow and wrench him free.

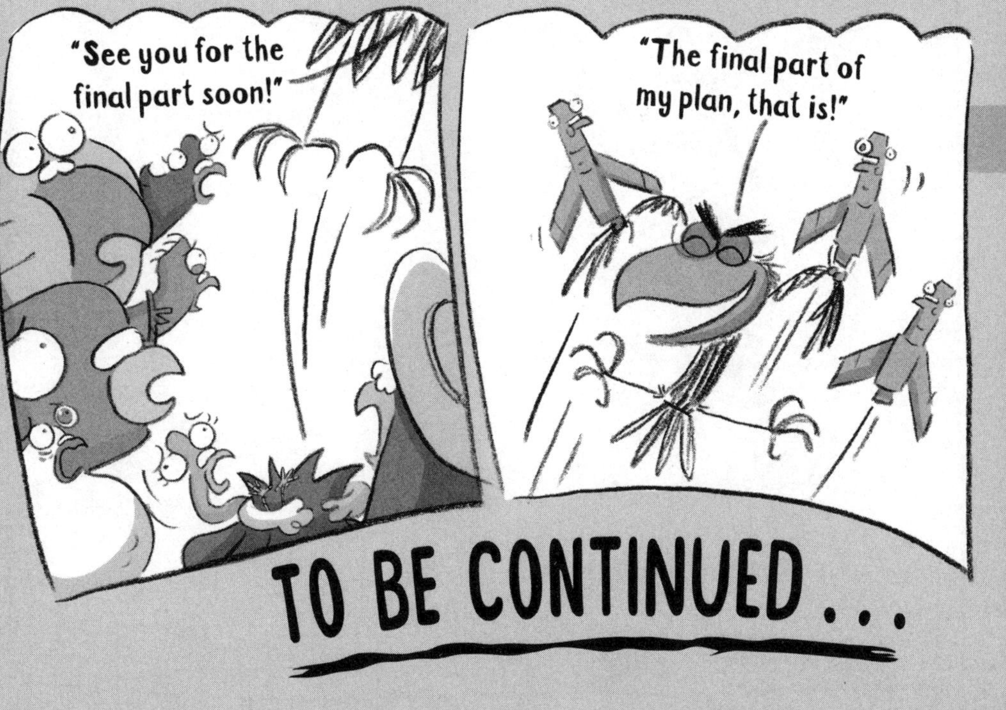
"See you for the final part soon!"
"The final part of my plan, that is!"
TO BE CONTINUED . . .

PART THREE THE VANISHING TREE

lovely leaves

spiky sticks

foggy fog

139

CHAPTER 1

Rock Pigeon is outside a fruit shop.

"Hello, pidgey!"

A kind human throws him some grapes.

He sticks his toes in them and walks off!

Grapes make pretty comfy shoes.

Rock isn't alone.

He is joined by the real Barb Pigeon and Kakapo.

"Grape shoes are so fancy!" says Barb.

"Grapes make walking feel like dancing," says Kakapo.

They are taking grapes back to share with the other **REAL PIGEONS**. Until they pass some . . .

Rock doesn't like crows.

But he isn't worried.

Until some shadows swoop down.

It's Jungle Crow.

The **REAL PIGEONS'** number one enemy.

And he has three pigeon robots with him.

"There they are!" he cries with glee. "Get them, **PIGBOTS!**"

Rock, Barb, and Kakapo try to run.

But the grapes burst.

SPLAT!

SPLAT!

SPLAT!

SPLAT!

144

The birds are surrounded.

"That's the crow who **IMPERSONATED** me!"

"You're not a person!"

"Then that's the crow who **IMPIGEON**ATED me!"

"What are you doing, Jungle Crow?" splutters Rock. "Why did you pretend to be Barb Pigeon? And where did all these ROBOT PIGEONS come from?"

"Impressive, aren't they!" says Jungle Crow. "All made from scrap metal. They're my new assistants."

drainpipe bodies

teaspoon beaks

car-antenna legs

Rock glares at the **PIGBOTS**. "Traitors."

"The **PIGBOTS** are helping with my **EVIL PLAN**," says Jungle Crow.

"**ANOTHER** evil plan?" cries Rock. "I hate you, Jungle Crow!"

"That's a bit mean, Rock, dear!" says Barb gently.

"Kakapo thought you loved **ALL** nature?"

Rock is shocked. "But Jungle Crow is **ALWAYS** out to get us. And he pretended to be you, Barb!"

"That was wrong," says Barb. "But have you ever tried being kind to him? Maybe he just needs a hug."

"I don't do hugs," Jungle Crow says. "I do **EVIL PLANS**. And when you find out what this plan is, you're not going to like it!"

Jungle Crow does an evil **LAUGH**.

"MWA HA HA!"

And an evil **CAW**.

"CAW CAW CAW!"

He is halfway through an evil **CACKLE** when a **PIGBOT** taps him on the shoulder.

"CACK—"

"Excuse. Me. Mr. Jungle. Crow."

"What?!"

The **PIGBOT'S** voice is like a beeping microwave. "Can. We. Please. Have. Some. Screws?"

Jungle Crow sighs and takes some metal screws from under his wing. "**PIGBOTS** don't eat bread crumbs. But they **LOVE** screws."

"Enough snacks!" shouts Jungle Crow. "Let's grab these birds and put them with the rest!"

149

But Rock, Barb, and Kakapo have vanished.

"Where. Did. The. Real. Pigeons. Go?"

Jungle Crow shrugs. "My **EVIL PLAN** will take care of them anyway."

He flies off with the **PIGBOTS**.

Rock, Barb, and Kakapo step out from their sleeping-man disguise.

"Kakapo thanks you for the loan."

"We need to find out what Jungle Crow's **EVIL PLAN** is and stop him," cries Rock. "Let's go!"

151

The three birds speed back to the gazebo.

"Squad!" says Rock. "We have a **BIRDMERGENCY!**"

He tells them everything.

"Jungle Crow will never beat us."

"So does this mean you didn't get any grapes?"

"That sounds terrible!" says Grandpouter.
"But we have another problem right here."

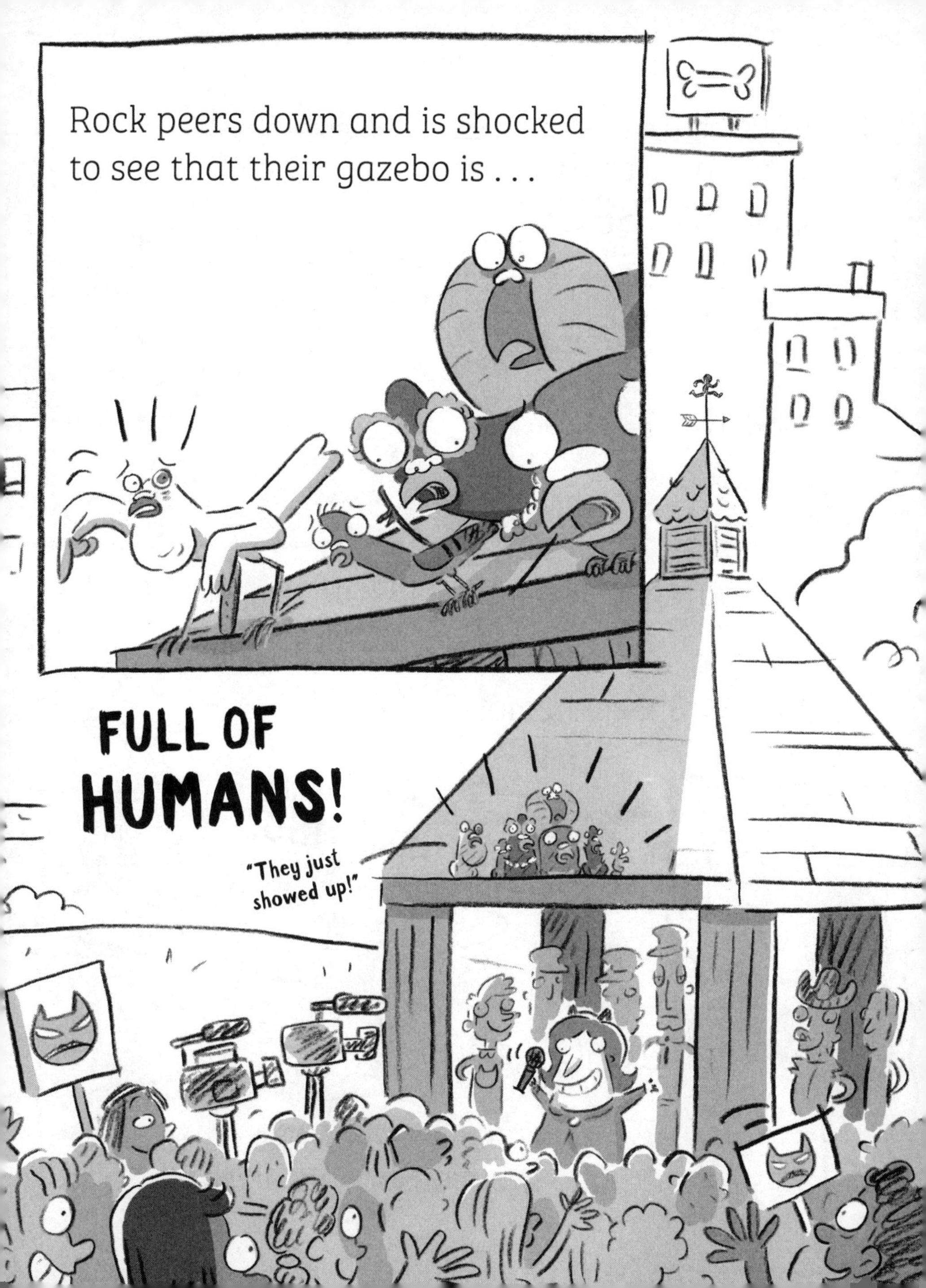
Rock peers down and is shocked to see that their gazebo is . . .
FULL OF HUMANS!
"They just showed up!"

Some kind of event is happening at the gazebo. With the woman from the **CAT MUSEUM.**

"I'm going to run for **CITY MAYOR!**"

Her name is Bertie Berd-Byrd.

The pigeons have met her before. She is afraid of . . .

"**BIRDS!** AHHHHHHHHHHH! HOW **TERRIFYING!**"

"Time to go!"

The pigeons fly to a pine tree. It's their favorite tree. Even though it's right beside the **CAT MUSEUM.**

"I'm so tired, my feathers are drooping."

"Let's spend the night here to be safe," says Grandpouter, yawning.

And the birds all go to sleep.

The next morning, Rock wakes up on the ground.

Along with the other birds.

"What happened to the tree?"

"Huh?"

They all look around in panic.

The tree has vanished!

Rock's eyes narrow.
He knows who did this.

"JUNGLE CROW!"

CHAPTER 2

The **REAL PIGEONS** are so confused.

"Where did our favorite tree go, **PIGS?**"

The sandbox is still there. So is the park bench. But the tree is gone. There's not even a stump left.

"How is this possible?" says Tumbler.

"Jungle Crow and the **PIGBOTS** must have stolen our tree," says Rock. "Maybe this is part of their **EVIL PLAN!**"

"We have a new mission," says Grandpouter.

"REAL PIGEONS FIND VANISHED TREES!"

Kakapo is confused by all the leaping and yelling. But he likes it. So he does a leap of his own.

"KAKAPO SHOUTING WORDS, WOOHOO!"

Rock is worried more trees might go missing. So first, he visits his ibis friend.

"Hello, birdo—I just invented a sardine-tin phone!"

Straw Neck lives in a dumpster and invents things from garbage.

"I need some help," says Rock. "Can you invent something to stop trees from being stolen out of the ground?"

Straw Neck digs through the dumpster.

"People throw away the strangest things," she says. "But these should do the trick!"

She has invented . . .

TREE ANCHORS!

"Perfect!" says Rock, flying off. "Now we just need to find the pine tree that vanished."

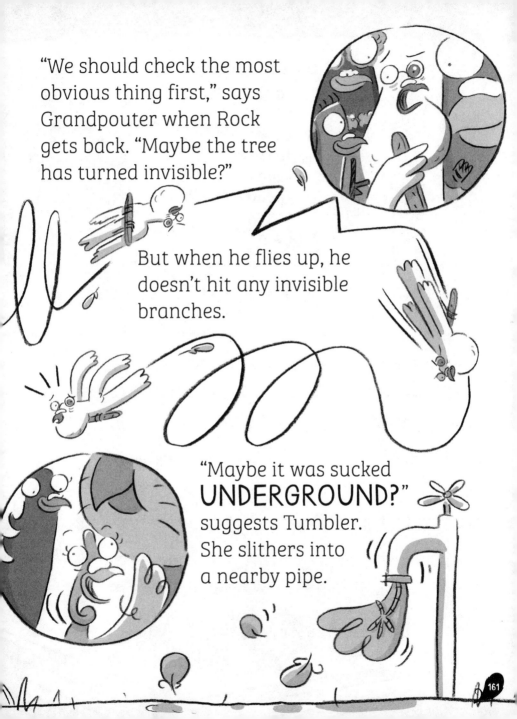

"We should check the most obvious thing first," says Grandpouter when Rock gets back. "Maybe the tree has turned invisible?"

But when he flies up, he doesn't hit any invisible branches.

"Maybe it was sucked **UNDERGROUND?**" suggests Tumbler. She slithers into a nearby pipe.

But all she finds is their friend Rattus.

"Hi, Tumbler! Look, I've stretched my tail to spell out words so humans will know rats aren't scary."

dont scream

Barb Pigeon and Kakapo visit the lumber yard. There are no freshly cut down trees. But someone *is* waiting for them.

"Shall we rest and eat a tea bag?"

"YES! What's a tea bag?"

Frillback checks inside the **CAT MUSEUM.**

But after searching, she decides there is nothing in there but old cat history.

KING TUTANCATMAN

EXIT

The tree has vanished without a trace!

"We'll just have to comb the area for clues," says Grandpouter.

The pigeons borrow some combs from a hairdresser.

And start by combing the grass.

"Where did all the combs go?"

164

Rock is busy combing when he has another idea. "Maybe Jungle Crow took the tree with him?" he says.

Grandpouter nods. "Try to find out while we keep combing."

"OK, bye!"

Rock circles above the city. He soon sees **JUNGLE CROW** and the **PIGBOTS** standing on a corner.

"We. Want. More. Screws. To. Eat!"

"Where is the missing pine tree?" Rock shouts. "We know you stole it."

"Huh?" says Jungle Crow, looking stressed. "Go away. I'm busy looking for screws. Even though I don't want to."

"But. You. Promised."

"So. Not. Fair."

"Screws! Screws! Screws!"

Rock is about to argue.

Until he remembers what Barb and Kakapo said about being kind.

166

So he offers Jungle Crow some advice.

"We get bread crumbs by standing outside a bakery," he says. "If you stand outside a hardware store, maybe you'll get screws?"

Jungle Crow's beak goes wobbly.

"Are you *helping* me?"

He is not used to a pigeon being nice to him.

But he does what Rock says.

And before long, it works.

"Hooray!"

CLINK
CLINK
CLINK
CLINK
CLINK

A human throws the **PIGBOTS** some screws.

HARDWARE

"What are you doing, Frank?"

"I could have sworn these birds were begging for screws!"

CRUNCH
CRUNCH
CRUNCH

"Now will you tell me where the pine tree is?" says Rock.

But Jungle Crow just laughs.
"You must be very careless
to lose a tree. I'd be more
worried about Barb and
Kakapo if I were you!"

Meanwhile, in a big hole under a picnic
blanket and a fake family . . .

"I can't believe
Jungle Crow has trapped
us all down here!"
says Barb.

"We're just happy
to see you, real Barb!"

Rock is shocked. "Where did you take them?"

"I **BIRDNAPPED** them, along with all the other city pigeons!" says Jungle Crow. "And **YOU'RE NEXT.**"

"Now get him, PIGBOTS!"

"HEY!"

Luckily, the **PIGBOTS** are still munching on screws, so Rock quickly escapes. He's really worried about Barb and Kakapo.

"How will we stop Jungle Crow this time?"

Rock stops by the fruit shop. A yummy grape will help him figure out what to do next.

But Bertie Berd-Byrd is there. She throws a rotten tomato at him.

"Pigeons are horrible pests!"

HOW TO VOTE

Rock is frustrated. And very tomato-y.

"I haven't found the tree yet," he mutters.

"Being kind to Jungle Crow was useless. And now Kakapo, Barb, and all the city pigeons are trapped somewhere!"

Suddenly, Rock stops moaning.

A **PIGBOT** is scooting past.

"Now **THAT** gives me an idea," whispers Rock. "I'll just need some help."

A few minutes later, the **PIGBOT** comes across a **GIANT** screw sitting in a hole in a wall.

"This. Is. The. Best. Thing. That. Has. Ever. Happened. Except. For. The. First. Time. My. ON. Button. Was. Pressed."

The **PIGBOT** is about to eat the screw.

Except . . . it's not a screw.

It's Tumbler. She's twisty like a screw.

She quickly slips out of the hole—

"Bye!"

as Frillback and Homey slam their combs over it.

The **PIGBOT** is trapped in comb jail!

"Yesss!"

The pigeons try to get the **PIGBOT** to talk.

"I'll ask you again," says Rock. "Where are Kakapo, Barb, and the other pigeons? And did you and Jungle Crow steal our pine tree?"

But the **PIGBOT** refuses.

"No. Comment."

"If you're going to be like that," says Rock, "we'll take you to someone who can get machines to talk."

They carry the **PIGBOT** to the dumpster.

Straw Neck peers down her long beak. "Oh my gosling," she says. "You have one of my robot pigeons!"

Rock is gobsmacked. "**YOU** invented the **PIGBOTS**, Straw Neck?"

"Yes!" she says. "They are my babies."

"Straw. Neck?"

"That's Mommy Straw Neck to you!"

"Their brains are old microchips," she says. "Their hearts are flashlight batteries. And I made them always hungry—just like real pigeons!"

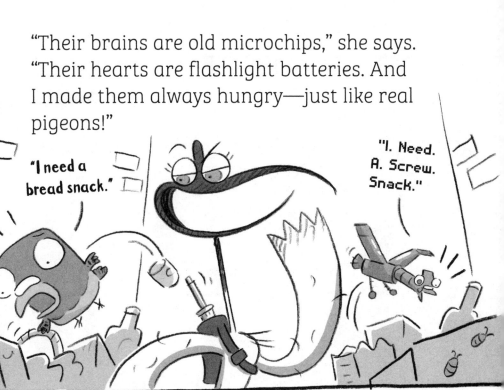

"I need a bread snack."

"I. Need. A. Screw. Snack."

"Are you working with Jungle Crow?" says Rock, poking Trent at the ibis.

"No," says Straw Neck. "I created the **PIGBOTS** to help me invent things. But they were stolen before I could switch them on."

"I found a bag of screws!" says Homey.
"Maybe now the **PIGBOT** will talk."

Rock marches up to the **PIGBOT**.
"If you want to eat these screws, tell us
EVERYTHING."

The **PIGBOT** explains immediately.

Jungle Crow stole the **PIGBOTS** one day when Straw Neck wasn't looking.

"MWAHA HA!"

Then he dressed up like Barb Pigeon.

"Hello, dears!"

"We love you, Barb."

"I know you do. . . . I mean, I love you too, pigeons."

He dug a big hole in the park and covered it with a picnic blanket and a fake family. Then he tricked all the city pigeons into it!

"Sure, we'll go down here. We trust you, Barb!"

Jungle Crow didn't want any crime-fighting pigeons to interfere with his EVIL PLAN.

The plan is for **PIGBOTS** to steal the city's best food and give it to all the crows.

"But what about our missing tree?" says Rock.

"That. Was. Not. Us," says the **PIGBOT**.

Homey feeds the **PIGBOT**.

"Thanks for chatting, now for snacking!"

"CRUNCH!"

As Rock wonders who else would steal a tree, Frillback flies off. "I'm going to rescue the pigeons and Kakapo," she says.

Frillback finds a picnic.

Flies straight into it.

And gets whacked by a man holding a baguette.

"Oops! Wrong picnic!" she says.

It turns out there are LOTS of picnics happening.

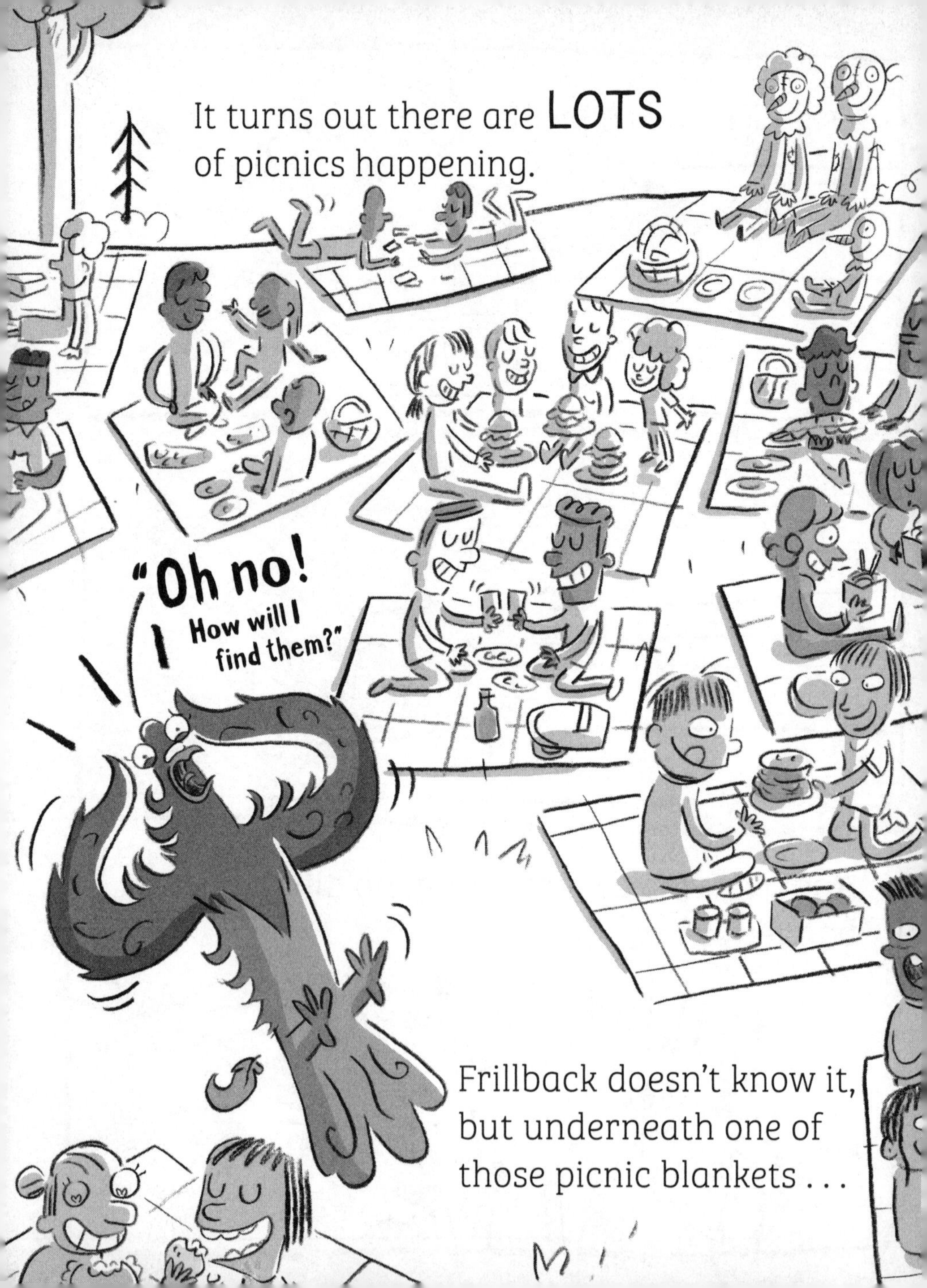
"Oh no!
How will I find them?"

Frillback doesn't know it, but underneath one of those picnic blankets . . .

[redacted]
trapped city pigeons to have a

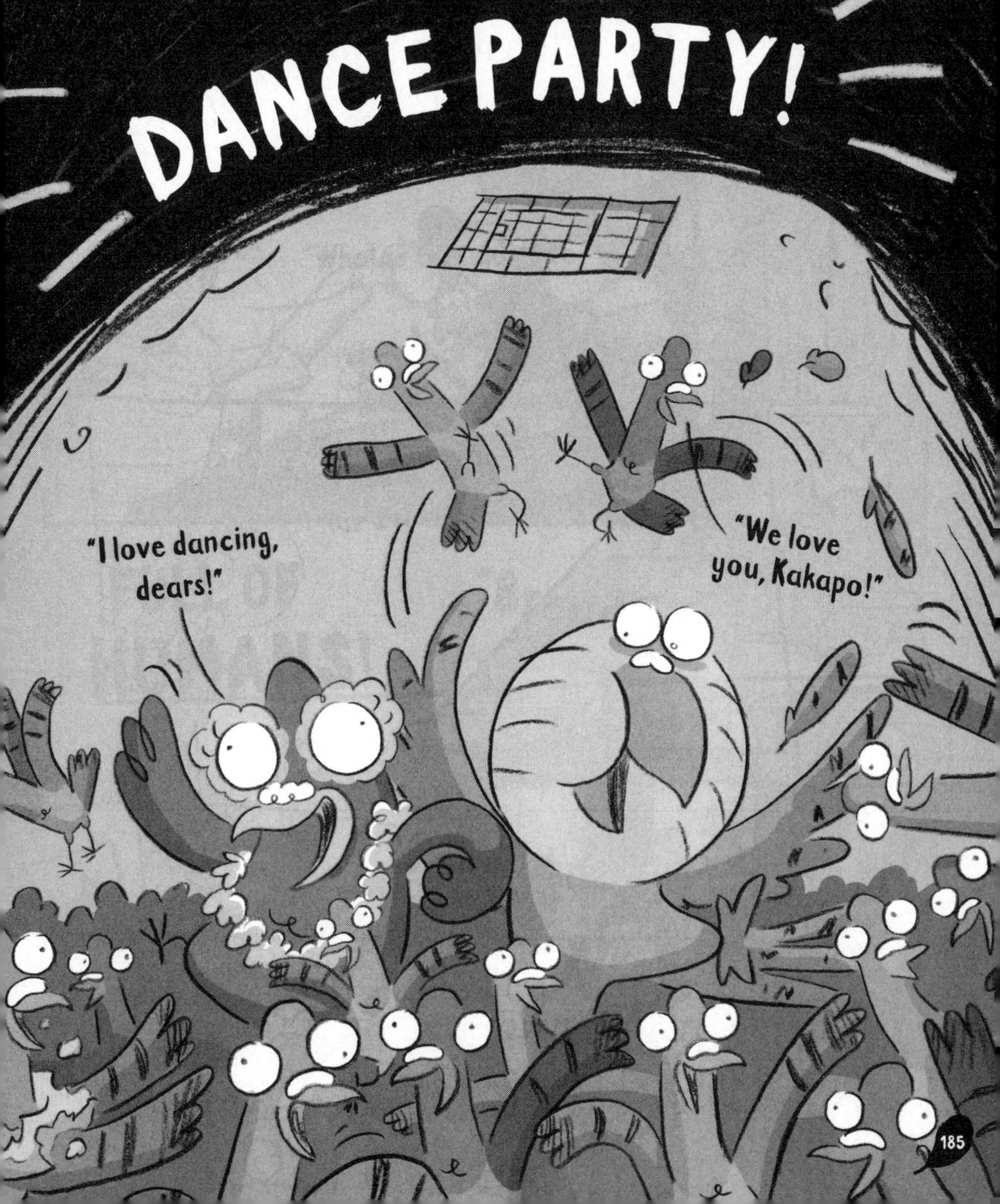
DANCE PARTY!
"I love dancing, dears!"
"We love you, Kakapo!"

Meanwhile, back at the dumpster . . .

"Do you want your **PIGBOT** back?" Tumbler asks Straw Neck. "It can help with inventing."

Before Straw Neck can answer, the **PIGBOT** spins around.

"**No!**" it says.

"Pigbots. Don't. Want.
To. Be. Inventors.
Pigbots. Just. Want.
To. Be. Rocket. Ships."

"Oh," says Straw Neck, surprised.

"But. Only. The. Best. Metal.
Is. Used. In. Rockets,"
moans the PIGBOT.
"Not. Scraps. Like. Us."

Homey offers the PIGBOT
another screw. "You're not a scrap," he says.

"Thank. You.
Square. Pigeon."

But then they both cough and splutter.

"Ew, I ate a screw!"

"Ew. I. Ate.
A. Bread."

Homey mixed up the snacks.

While Homey and the **PIGBOT** recover . . .

"Drink a cup of water."

"Drink a cup of engine oil."

. . . Rock thinks hard. "We still don't know who stole the tree!" he says. "If Jungle Crow didn't take it, who did?"

"Are you missing a tree, birdo?" says Straw Neck. "Someone dropped some branches behind my dumpster last night."

"No way!" cries Tumbler.

"Yes way!"

The pigeons fly around and stare at the freshly cut branches.

"It's the top of the pine tree!" cries Homey.

Rock shakes his head. "Where's the rest of it?" He looks into the distance. "There's a trail of wood shavings over there. Let's follow it!"

"They're called TREE CRUMBS!"

The pigeons follow the tree crumbs, finding Grandpouter on the way.

"I've been combing this whole time!"

The tree-crumb trail leads the Real Pigeons back to the **CAT MUSEUM.**

Where they find . . .

. . . NOTHING!

"There's no tree," groans Homey, looking around. "It must have been chopped into a million crumbs!"

Rock looks up. "Frillback checked *inside* the museum. But . . ."

Suddenly, he understands.

"Our tree hasn't been all cut up!" he cries. "And I know where it is."

CHAPTER 4

Before Rock can explain where the missing tree is, they hear a rumbling.

Tumbler bends her ear to the ground. "What's that noise?"

RUMBLE RUMBLE

It's bad news.

Jungle Crow and the **PIGBOTS** come flapping around the corner . . .

. . . chased by a crowd of angry humans!

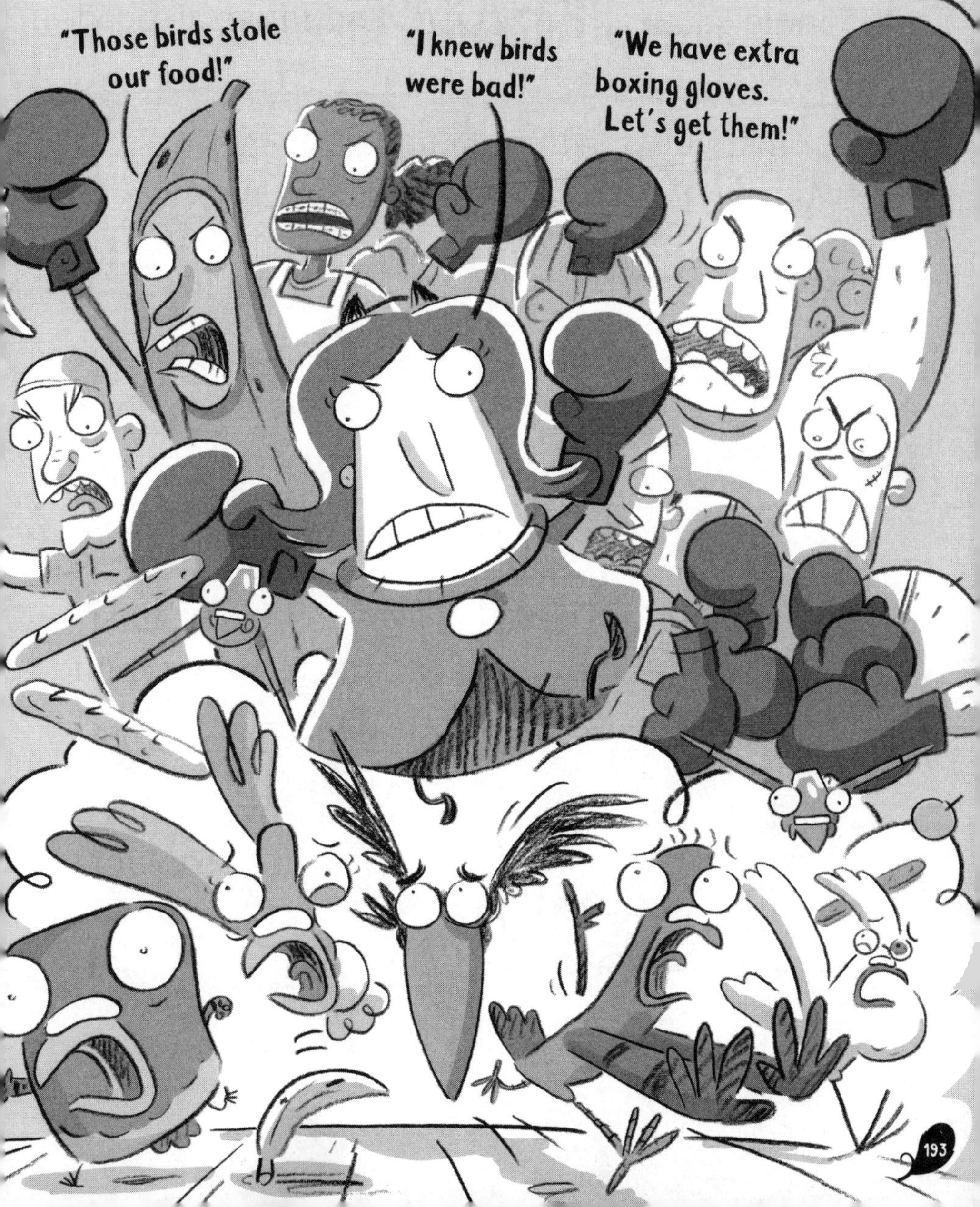
"Those birds stole our food!"
"I knew birds were bad!"
"We have extra boxing gloves. Let's get them!"

"My **EVIL PLAN** has backfired," shouts Jungle Crow. "**PIGBOTS!** Fight the humans!"

But instead of leaping into action, the last two **PIGBOTS** cross their wings stubbornly.

But Jungle Crow doesn't **HAVE** any more screws.

The boxing humans start swinging punches.

"Now I have you, **DIRTY** pigeons!" sneers Bertie Berd-Byrd.

Suddenly, Frillback returns from the picnics and coos above all the noise.

"**REAL PIGEONS PECK PUNCHES!**"

And so they do.

Bertie and the humans punch at the pigeons.
And the pigeons peck back.

A stray punch goes through a wall. And Rock sees something amazing. "We've got to tear down this wall!" he shouts.

PUNCH.
PECK!

PUNCH.
PECK!

PUNCH.
PECK!

PUNCH.
PECK!

He flies over to the **PIGBOTS**, who are still on strike.

"I know where you can find more screws," he says.

The **PIGBOTS** fly over to the **CAT MUSEUM**.

And start greedily pulling out the screws.

The building shakes.

The **PIGBOTS** flee with two giant wingfuls of screws.

"You. Were. Right. There. Were. Heaps. Here."

Rock winces as the building's walls start to fall. Everyone is so busy fighting that they don't notice—until it's too late!

"UH-OH!"

"RETREAT!"

"WHO WILL SAVE US?!"

Meanwhile, the **UNDERGROUND DANCE PARTY** is shaking the earth so much that it crumbles.

The picnic blanket with the fake family caves in!

"Kakapo's dance party has saved us, dears!"

And the birds fly free.

Straightaway, they see danger at the **CAT MUSEUM**.

The city pigeons swoop in to save the day, catching all the walls.

The humans cheer.

"Sorry we hated you back there. We got carried away."

"Would you look at that!" hoots Grandpouter. "That building was fake!"

The pigeons look up and see . . . the pine tree!

"Hooray, our tree is back!"

"The tree was never stolen," says Rock.
"Or chopped down. Bertie Berd-Byrd just
tricked us into thinking it was gone!"

Bertie is fuming.

"Boo, hiss!" she says. "Just
FOR ONCE I wanted
a tree without any birds
in it. I'll get you birds, if it's
the last thing I do!"

no birds
here

or here

how heavenly

Rock explains how she made the tree
VANISH.

"Bertie Berd-Byrd's builders must have built the fake building overnight," he says. "And moved the sandbox and the park bench so it looked like the tree had vanished."

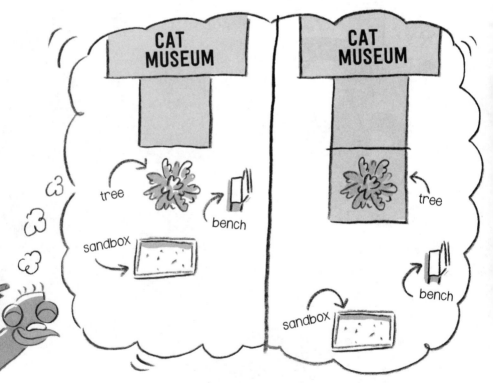

Rock is feeling very proud of himself. And doesn't see Bertie Berd-Byrd coming.

She has made a
GIANT BOXING GLOVE.

She swings it straight at Rock.

"Take that, dirty pigeon!"

But Jungle Crow suddenly swoops into Rock.

And Bertie Berd-Byrd punches the ground.

"GRRR! I missed. This would have really hurt if I wasn't wearing lots of boxing gloves!"

Rock blinks at Jungle Crow in disbelief. "You . . . saved me?" he says.

Jungle Crow shrugs. "You helped me get screws before, so . . ."

Rock smiles. Barb and Kakapo were right. Kindness worked!

"Thank you!"

"Don't mention it. Seriously, I don't want anyone knowing I was nice to a pigeon."

The pigeons fly up to the old pine tree and find Barb and Kakapo.

"There you are!"

"The tree is back!" Grandpouter smiles. "And even though the **CAT MUSEUM** is right there, we can finally relax."

"We can try, anyway!" Rock grins.

THE END

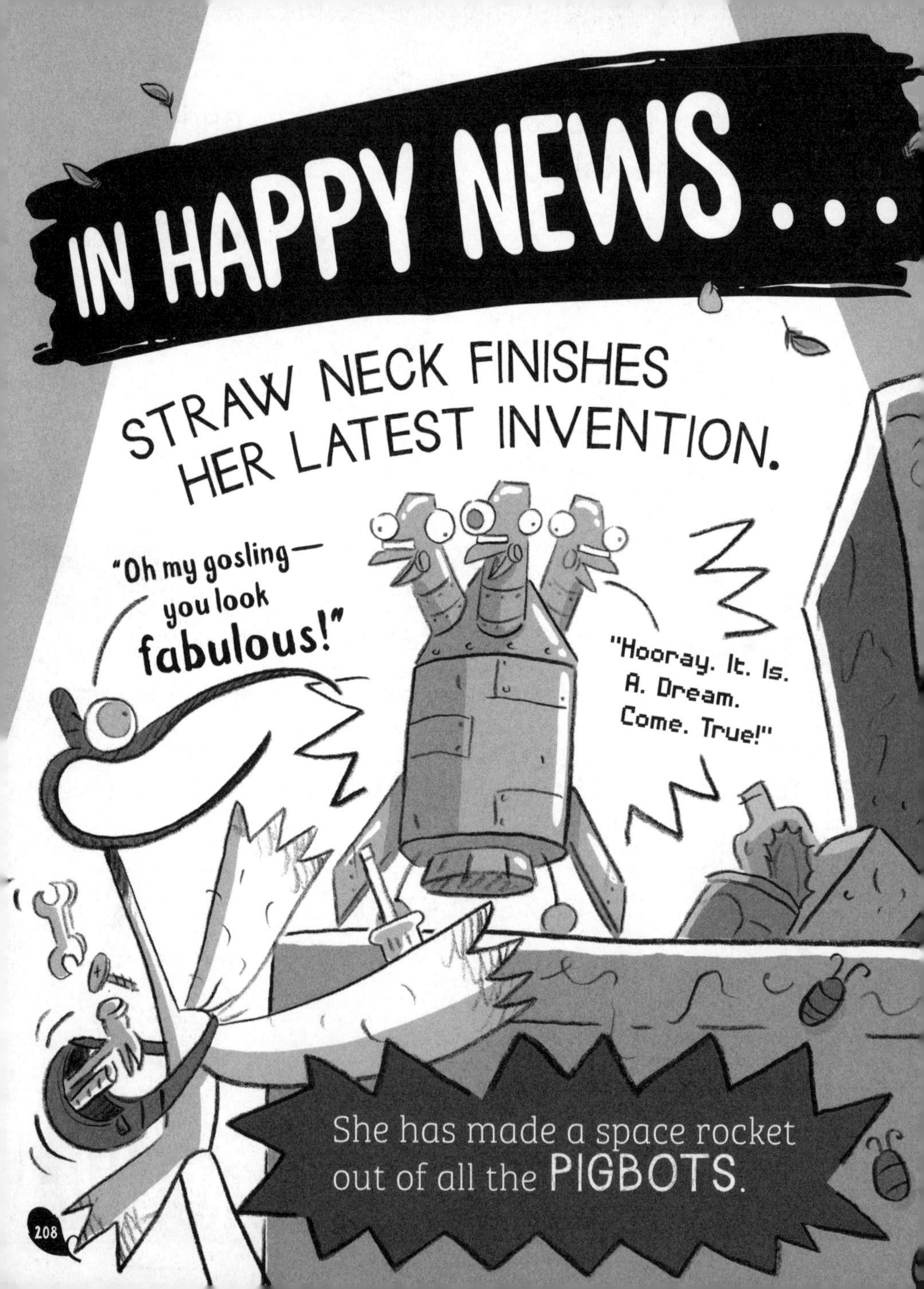
IN HAPPY NEWS . . .
STRAW NECK FINISHES HER LATEST INVENTION.
"Oh my gosling—you look fabulous!"
"Hooray. It. Is. A. Dream. Come. True!"
She has made a space rocket out of all the PIGBOTS.

The **PIGBOTS** take off.

FWOOM!

And live happily ever after in space.

209

IN UNHAPPY NEWS ...

BERTIE BERD-BYRD HAS JUST BECOME THE MAYOR.

Because she was the only candidate.

She makes her first speech.

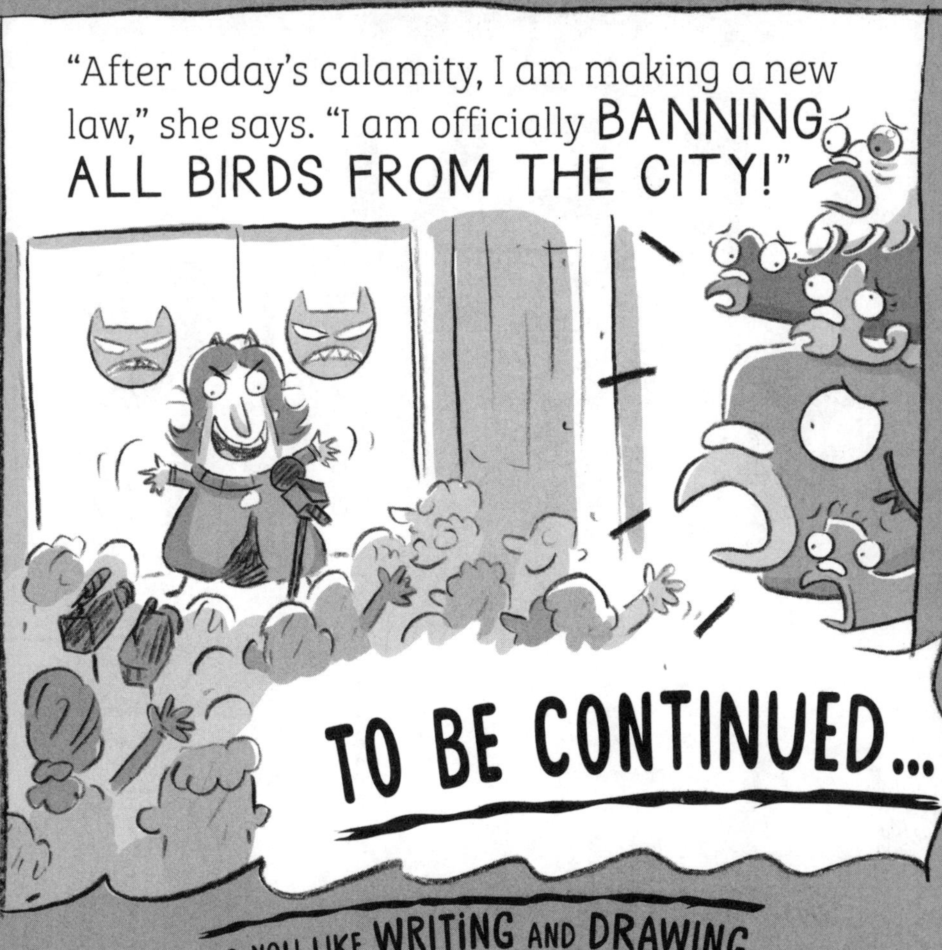
"After today's calamity, I am making a new law," she says. "I am officially BANNING ALL BIRDS FROM THE CITY!"
TO BE CONTINUED...

DO YOU LIKE **WRITING** AND **DRAWING** AND **SILLINESS** AND **PIGEONS?**

JOIN THE CLUB AT **REALPIGEONS.COM!**

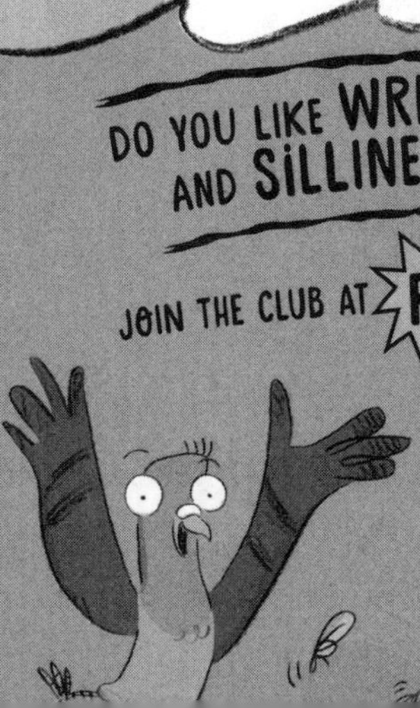

Join Andrew and Ben in **THE SUPER COO CLUB** to watch videos, learn how to draw the REAL PIGEONS, write silly stories—plus MORE!

DID YOU KNOW

REAL PIGEONS

ARE

REAL-LIFE

PIGEONS?

ROCK PIGEON

The most common pigeon in the world. Gray with two black stripes on each wing. Very good at blending in!

FRILLBACK PIGEON

Known as a "fancy pigeon." Humans have bred them to be covered in curly feathers. These birds don't need to use hair curlers!

TUMBLER PIGEON

Known to tumble or somersault while in flight. They fly normally before unexpectedly doing aerial acrobatics.

HOMING PIGEON

Has the incredible ability to fly long distances and return home from very far away. They were used to deliver letters many years ago.

POUTER PIGEON

The big bubble that looks like a chest is actually called a crop. They store food in their crops before releasing it to their stomachs. Yuck!

FIND OUT MORE AT REALPIGEONS.COM!

MORE REAL-LIFE CREATURES!

KAKAPO

The kakapo is one of the world's most **endangered birds**. Kakapos used to be found everywhere in New Zealand until predators, like cats and weasels, were introduced. Now there are just a few hundred left on some small islands.

Kakapos are nocturnal parrots that can't fly. They live on a vegetarian diet consisting of fruit, moss, and ferns. They have big personalities and have even been dubbed "party parrots." But they freeze in the face of danger, which is less of a party.

To find out more or make a donation to help conservation efforts, visit **KAKAPORECOVERY.ORG.NZ**

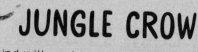

JUNGLE CROW

A bird with an incredibly large beak, the jungle crow is big and bossy in real life too! Jungle crows go to any lengths for a snack and are considered pests. They're also quite rude.

BARB PIGEON

Barb pigeons are a kind of fancy pigeon that have a lumpy, red growth around the eyes. This might look odd until you realize the red growth looks like a flower. Barbs are pretty flower birds!

ERMINE

Weasels are fierce predators that lurk, hunt, and eat small creatures. There are multiple weasel species, and they're also called stoats and ermines. That's where Ermine gets his name.

A GUIDE TO USING
MORSE COODE

Send and receive SECRET MESSAGES using MORSE COODE— a special language only pigeons use. When writing in Morse coode, make sure you use a full stop after each letter.

A:	Coo cooo	N:	Cooo coo
B:	Cooo coo coo coo	O:	Cooo cooo cooo
C:	Cooo coo cooo coo	P:	Coo cooo cooo coo
D:	Cooo coo coo	Q:	Cooo cooo coo cooo
E:	Coo	R:	Coo cooo coo
F:	Coo coo cooo coo	S:	Coo coo coo
G:	Cooo cooo coo	T:	Cooo
H:	Coo coo coo coo	U:	Coo coo cooo
I:	Coo coo	V:	Coo coo coo cooo
J:	Coo cooo cooo cooo	W:	Coo cooo cooo
K:	Cooo coo cooo	X:	Cooo coo coo cooo
L:	Coo cooo coo coo	Y:	Cooo coo cooo cooo
M:	Cooo cooo	Z:	Cooo cooo coo coo

Use **MORSE COODE** to decode this message from the **REAL PIGEONS!**

Cooo cooo coo. Cooo cooo cooo.

Cooo cooo cooo. Cooo coo coo.

Coo cooo coo coo. Coo coo cooo.

Cooo coo cooo coo. Cooo coo cooo.

Coo cooo cooo coo. Coo coo.

Cooo cooo coo. Coo coo coo.

Write the message here:

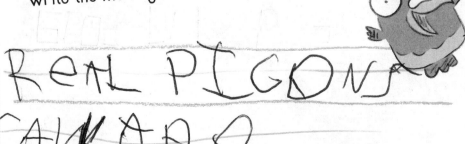

REAL PIGONS
AVKAPO